## The Beginning

"What are you *doing?*" I heard myself scream hysterically.

Dad glared at me over his shoulder, as if the hole in the wall were my fault. I ran up to my room and locked the door behind me.

I don't think — no, I *know* I didn't sleep that night. I'd never been so scared in my life. Oh, sure, I was afraid of the usual stuff. Like getting killed in a car accident, or dying from some horrid disease while I was still pretty young — like Debra Winger in *Terms of Endearment*. But I'd never, *never* been afraid to be in the same house with my own family. And the way I felt now, I was thinking there wasn't anything worse.

Only, then, I didn't know that this was just the beginning.

Other Scholastic books
you will enjoy:

*Fallen Angels*
by Walter Dean Myers

*Long Live the Queen*
by Ellen Emerson White

*Probably Still Nick Swansen*
by Virginia Euwer Wolff

*Paradise Lane*
by William Taylor

*The Tricksters*
by Margaret Mahy

*Sheila's Dying*
by Alden R. Carter

YA
Jen

point

# POCKET CHANGE

## Kathryn Jensen

WITHDRAWN

Middlebury Public Library

SCHOLASTIC INC.
New York Toronto London Auckland Sydney

No part of this publication may be reproduced in whole or in part, or stored in a retrieval system, or transmitted in any form or by any means, electronic, mechanical, photocopying, recording, or otherwise, without written permission of the publisher. For information regarding permission write to Macmillan Publishing Company, 866 Third Avenue, New York, NY 10022.

ISBN 0-590-43419-5

Copyright © 1989 by Kathryn Jensen. All rights reserved. Published by Scholastic Inc., 730 Broadway, New York, NY 10003, by arrangement with Macmillan Publishing Company. POINT is a registered trademark of Scholastic Inc.

12 11 10 9 8 7 6 5 4 3 2                    1 2 3 4 5/9

Printed in the U.S.A.                                          01

First Scholastic printing, December 1990

For their selflessly given time, advice, and support throughout the writing of this book, I wish to thank the following people: James Jensen, Linda Hayes, Phyllis Larkin, Bette Barton, M.D. (former Medical Rating Specialist for the Veterans Administration), Raymond M. Scurfield, D.S.W. (National Assistant Director for Counseling, Readjustment Counseling Service, Veterans Administration), Jerry Atchison (Disabled American Veterans), John Welch, David Hoang, JoAnn Tater; and Ruth Glick, Nancy Baggett, and Chassie West, as well as other members of the Columbia Writer's Workshop. Whatever is real and accurate in this story is due to their effort. Any errors are mine.

*To Margaret and Rufus Kimball*

# CHAPTER ONE

THINK NOVEMBER, UP NORTH . . . NEW ENGLAND. THINK favorite hangout scenes, places you go to blow off steam. I'll take you to mine and start from there. Because that is where I spent the last few minutes of my life that made any sense for a long, long time . . .

BRIAN RAISED THE BUTT OF THE BROWNING SHOTGUN to his shoulder and leveled his eyes along the black, metal barrel. "Pull!" he shouted.

I released the trap and a clay disk sprang into the cool, crisp Connecticut air above Riveredge Rod & Gun Club. The gun's crack split the afternoon's silence, but the target continued untouched on its graceful arc, landing in a clump of brown marsh grass.

"Want to shoot another rotation?" I called.

"Forget it." Brian ejected the spent shells and tucked the Browning between his ribs and elbow, barrel pointed at the ground even though it was no longer loaded. He looked disgusted, his smooth brown hair slanting across his forehead and one eye.

I moved over to walk in his shadow. "You've been shooting less than a year," I said. But that sounded as if I was making excuses for him. I looped my wrist around his and we held hands, his shoulder a good four inches higher than mine. "Maybe my gun is too short for you. Your arms are longer than mine."

"Yeah, maybe."

"Ask for a trap gun for Christmas."

He laughed at that. "A cop's kid? Doubt it, Josie."

1

"But your dad knows you come to Riveredge with me."

"He doesn't mind if I learn to shoot. He just doesn't want a gun in the house. Besides his."

I unzipped the gun bag we'd left on the bench. It had "Josephine Monroe" stenciled in dense, black ink along one canvas seam. A whiff of metal and gun oil hit my nose when I pulled open the flaps. That smell always made me feel good inside, the way other people get all mellow about brownies or homemade bread baking. There'd been about seven years between the time my real mother left and Marsha, my stepmother, came to live with us. Dad and I hardly ever used the oven, then. We had sandwiches, or ate out. But we went shooting every Wednesday, and on Tuesday nights, to get ready, we'd spread newspapers across the living room carpet and sit together, cleaning our guns.

Standing back a step, I watched the muscles of Brian's shoulders work gently under his blue-and-rust-plaid flannel shirt as he put the Browning to bed. Spiky, tan hairs ran in matched paths up the back of his neck from the collar. That always makes me smile, noticing little things about him. I like being near Bri. We've been going together almost a whole year now — our first date was January 21, 1986. Sometimes getting to see each other is hard to manage, since he lives across the river in New London, and I'm in Groton. But when it happens, I like it. A lot.

"*You* did great today," he said over his shoulder. Brian dropped the leftover cartridges into the pocket on the front of the bag and snapped it closed.

"I was six years old the first time I shot," I told him.

"Really?" He sounded surprised but also kind of relieved.

2

"You do something for ten years, you get good."

"Not always," he said, starting to walk toward the car. "But it helps, I suppose."

I could tell he was feeling better though. He bought two Pepsis from the machine outside the scorekeeper's shack, and we sat in his mother's green Pinto, with the engine running, the heat on. He cracked a window at the top, just in case. You know how you read about carbon monoxide fumes, and all. Brian's very careful about a lot of things most people never bother about. And that's another thing I like about him. He makes me feel safe, like I don't have to watch out for myself quite as much when he's around.

I clamped the soda can between my knees, so I could rub the cold out of my fingers, and snuggled down into the Pinto's worn seat. It was the first week of November and the temperature always beats the calendar in Connecticut. Winter arrives a good month or more ahead of the official date.

On Halloween Marsha had made my little brother wear a ski jacket over his E.T. costume. Of course, when you've just turned three years old, that's the worst thing that can happen to you. You get all dressed up in one of those flimsy step-in costumes K Mart sells and a plastic mask — then some grown-up makes you wear a coat and the whole effect's totally ruined.

Chrissy had sniveled as I took his hand and we went out the door. Once I'd got him around the block, I let him unzip his jacket so it just hung over his shoulders.

"Get a load of that jerk," said Brian.

I looked up, forgetting about Chrissy. Brian pointed out the windshield at a gray-haired guy in a down hunting vest. He was at the third of five shooting stations on the twenty-five-shot course.

"He looks real determined," I said. Like he was practicing for the real thing. You could see him mouthing curses when he missed the clay "pigeon." "I don't think I ever want to shoot live birds."

Brian finished off his drink with a single, long swallow. "Yeah, well. You don't have to kill anything if you don't want to." He crushed both cans between the heels of his hands. Cranking his window farther down, he lofted one, then the other, into a rusting oil drum.

"So, what do I do?" he asked.

I knew he'd gone back to talking shooting. There are times I think we're psychic, or something. He can start in the middle of an idea, and I'll know exactly where he's at. Or the other way around. I guess it'd be spooky if you were sitting there listening to us. But it makes me happy to know we can talk like that, without spelling out every word.

"I don't know," I said. "Your stance is right. Breathing's fine." I thought a minute. "I wish Dad could have come today. He learned to shoot in the army. Taught me. He'd know."

"Think he would? Come out with us, I mean."

I said automatically, "Of course he would. He likes you, Bri." But then, I thought about that. Not about my father approving of my boyfriend, but about my father. Him and me, actually.

Last year our every Wednesday shooting dates had gotten postponed more often than not, until we hardly ever went. Dad had turned into a super workaholic, spending lots of nights at the realty office, going in early weekdays. That meant he was hardly ever at home. Weekends had always been a lock because that's when realtors do most of their business anyway. People are off from work and want to be driven around to a dozen houses in one day. For as long as I can remember, he'd come home wiped out on Sundays. But now, he was like that all the time.

"I can ask," I said as we drove down the dirt road away from Riveredge, and left it at that. I didn't want to disappoint him.

When we reached the Exxon and had to wait behind two cars for a self-service pump, I was finally ready to ask Brian a question I'd been working up to for three days. I glanced along the seat at him, but he was twisted around and staring out the side window.

"What's wrong?" I asked.

"Noth — Oh, there." He pointed across the blacktop to a pay phone. "Do you have to be home any special time?"

"No. So long as I have an hour to finish lit."

"Give a call. We'll grab a pizza."

I leaned over close to his cheek and sighed in a husky voice, like Marilyn Monroe in *Some Like It Hot*. "Let's do-o-o-o that. We'll take it down to the beach."

He leered at me. "So we can watch the submarine races over pepperoni and mozzarella?"

"If you're lucky, Pedersen!" I teased, back to my normal voice.

He grabbed for me and we kissed until the woman waiting behind us leaned on her horn. Brian jumped a mile and flushed bright red.

"Oh, great! Why didn't you tell me the car at the pump moved?"

"I was busy." I giggled and dug a quarter out of my jeans pocket. He filled the tank while I phoned Marsha.

Everyone parks at Eastern Point when the beach is closed for the season. And, believe it or not, there actually are submarines. No races, of course. The navy

5

has a base about three miles up the Thames River, and now and then one of the nuclear subs will pass by. So they really are there to watch, gliding out to sea like great gray whales, their engines grumbling softly. But, mostly, no one at Eastern Point pays them much attention.

We split the cost of a large pizza with onions, sausage, and green peppers. Brian bought one jumbo soda, no ice. It'd stay plenty cold without, and one cup was easier to manage while climbing over rocks in the dark.

That night the beach wasn't crowded, only five cars in the whole place. One hand raised over his head like a high-class waiter, Brian balanced the thin cardboard box. We clambered over the salt-and-pepper granite, tinged in patches with slippery green kelp, until we'd got out to the point and our boulder. We sat there, watching the sun go down, his arm stretched out behind me, me leaning back against him.

Nothing can be better, I thought, feeling toasty inside in spite of the wind. The pizza got cold fast but tasted great anyway, mixed with salt spray. My nose numbed up after ten minutes.

From the other side of the river, the streetlights of New London, where Brian lived, drew slim, silver lines across the wave tops. A mile or so up from us, a ribbon of red and yellow headlights arched across Memorial Bridge, looking like a snake with no head, no tail. Just going on forever.

I licked tomato sauce from my fingers. "I'm glad we have some more time," I began.

"Oh, yeah?" Even in the dark I could tell Brian was leering again.

"No, really." I laughed. "I wanted to ask you something." I waited and he didn't say anything so I went on. "A girl in my class, Michelle Vonnegut, is having a party Friday."

"So?"

"So . . ." This was harder than I'd expected. I glanced up over my shoulder at his face. "So, we're invited."

He didn't take his eyes off the river. "We?"

"Well . . ." I snatched up a fourth slice of pizza. Nerves do that to me; I get ravenous. "I'm invited. And Michelle said I could bring a date. She knows we're going together, so I'm sure it's all right."

He laughed softly and leaned back to brush the crumbs off his hands. The cold air slithered between us.

"Well?" I asked.

"Umm."

"Umm-yes, or umm-no?"

"I don't fit in with your friends," he said abruptly. "Go alone if you like."

I groaned. "Don't be a nerd, Pedersen!"

Brian folded the empty pizza box in fourths, one piece still inside, then stood. When he reached out a hand to pull me up, I ignored it and pushed off the rocks without his help.

He turned away and started walking while I stood there, hands on my hips, wanting to follow him but determined not to give in this time.

"Just because there were a couple of bad scenes . . ." I shouted into the wind. He didn't stop. I scrambled over the rocks after him. "Brian, knock it off! Don't be so damn stubborn!"

He gave a short laugh, but didn't sound very amused. "It never works, Josie. Cost me twenty bucks that night Craig stuck me for his whole table's tab at Harvey's."

Harvey's Hamburgers is where I work. Brian comes

to keep me company sometimes. But I know he doesn't feel comfortable there. Only Groton kids hang out at Harvey's, and Groton and New London don't mix. They're sort of like Harvard and Yale, Army and Navy, CBS and NBC; there's always been a rivalry between the two schools, which I suppose goes back to the fact that we've always played each other every Thanksgiving Day for our homecoming game. So it's a pretty big deal and emotions run awfully high.

Anyway, one night at Harvey's, Craig Bush, our quarterback, insisted that Brian sit with him and his friends and celebrate Groton's win over Ledyard High — which seemed okay. But then Craig arranged for one of his goons to distract Brian while the others walked out without paying, and Brian got stuck with the bill for the whole table.

"That wasn't very nice," I admitted. "But they were tanked up after the game."

"And what about the time I brought you to Ocean Beach?" he yelled over his shoulder.

I halted at the top of the rocks and watched while Brian stood in the dim glow of the parking lot lamps and unlocked the Pinto. The memory still stung. We were spending the day at the beach on the New London side of the river and decided to stick with a group from Brian's school. Once they found out I was from Groton, though, they made a point of dumping on me. Nothing outright nasty. Just subtle stuff like trying to get Brian talking about people I didn't know so I couldn't join in. And sharing sodas and suntan oil — but not with me. And changing radio stations just when I'd started snapping my fingers to an old song I really liked.

That was the only drawback to our relationship. Brian wasn't accepted at my school's dances and clubs, and everyone at his school hated my guts because of where I was from. After a couple of stabs at it, he'd said, "To hell with them. What do we need them for?" And we'd starting doing things on our own. So maybe that was why we'd gotten as close as we had.

While he got back in the car and reached across to unlatch the passenger side, I walked over slowly, climbed in, and sat on the seat close to my own door. We drove the quarter mile to Tyler Avenue without a word. I stared at my reflection in the sideview mirror: blond hair falling in breeze-blown salty straggles, gray eyes (almost silver) — my dad's eyes, everyone always said.

After we'd pulled into the drive behind the Seville, I looked down at my hands. It stank that Brian let people get to him. We missed out on a lot. Maybe if we hung in there, people would get used to us.

I murmured, "Not everyone is as dumb as Craig Bush."

"So give them another chance. Is that what you're saying?"

I nodded.

"All right," he agreed at last. "We'll go to the party. But I'm not sure it's the smartest move I've ever made."

As it turned out, we never found out if that was true.

# CHAPTER TWO

When you live with people for a very long time, you get to know what they'll do before they do it.

So, I *knew* Marsha and Dad would be sitting in the living room in front of the TV, each with a glass of

Taylor Lake Country white wine, when I let myself in. They wouldn't be watching any particular show, just using it to talk over, sort of the way I do my homework with the radio turned up loud enough to hear it next door. It blocks junk out nicely, like the fact we're in the approach path for Pilgrim Airlines, and they've just gotten cleared for jets.

But when I stuck my key in the front door after Brian drove off, it wasn't locked. And when I stepped inside, there wasn't a soul in the living room. The lights were all off. An uneasy feeling nibbled at the base of my back. I couldn't put a name to it, but it seemed real enough.

Marsha came downstairs while I was switching off the porch light and locking up for the night. She was wearing a peach-colored flannel nightgown that brushed her ankles. Her feet were bare, and her pretty, short, reddish hair fuzzed around her face, which looked lost without the terry sweat band she almost always wore — even when she wasn't doing aerobics.

"Hi," I said, puzzled. "Hope I didn't wake you."

She shook her head. "I was just reading. Uh . . ." She glanced at the door. "Let's leave this open for a bit. Okay, sweet?"

Crossing in front of me, she turned the button in the center of the brass knob.

I glanced at the stairs, then back at her, and frowned. Something was up. "Is Dad out?" But, I thought automatically, his car was in the drive. And Marsha's was parked on the curb.

Marsha gave me a hug and, leaving one arm around my waist, strolled us toward the kitchen. "He's taking a walk. Left his keys here. Want something to eat?" She opened the fridge and, dragging me along with

10

her, bent down to peer inside. "Carrot cake? Bowl of Jell-O?"

I guess if I were to describe Marsha to a stranger, I'd say she was dizzy — a nice dizzy though. Things that bother other people, like street crime and the national deficit or an outbreak of mumps at school, just don't faze her. She seems to shut out anything bad. Instead of worrying, she whips up a batch of homemade applesauce, spiced with cinnamon. Or, if things get really scary (like when she hears on the news about terrorists hijacking a plane and threatening to blow up all two hundred passengers), she'll bake eight or nine loaves of bread in one afternoon.

She's not very old. Marsha married Dad four years ago when she was just twenty-three. I suppose she's still kind of immature in some ways. Last fall her mother died in a car accident. While we were packing for the drive to Pennsylvania, Marsha acted as if it was a holiday: baking pies to take along, making a gourmet picnic for us to have on the road. Then, at the last minute, she called her sister and said Chrissy was sick. She never got to the funeral. For months afterward, we talked as if Nana Kanorski was still alive in PA. Marsha never saw her dead, so maybe that kept her alive in her own mind. It didn't hit her until her birthday when no card arrived from Nana. Then she cried for days. And after that she made seven different kinds of cookies.

That night was typical of her dizziness and preoccupation with food. I laughed at her. "I just finished half a large pizza," I reminded her. "I'm not hungry."

She let go of the refrigerator door. "Oh," she said, and grinned. "Of course not. I'd forgotten. How did it go?"

"Riveredge or the pizza?" I asked, plopping down on a kitchen chair.

"Oh," she said, sighing and waving a hand in the air, "just everything. Tell me how it all went, start to finish."

I frowned. "Do you feel all right?" She's no pumper as parents go. She likes to hear what I've been doing, sometimes. But she doesn't push for a blow-by-blow of every minute I'm out of her sight.

"I'm fine," she said, still looking somewhat distracted, and glanced toward the front door. "I was just curious about your night."

"Brian's getting pretty good," I told her, deciding to go along with the game. "When he remembers to do everything he should at the same time, he hits about fifty percent." Then, of course, I thought of my promise to him. "Think Dad would go out with us sometime soon? I know he could help Bri better than I can."

A thoughtful light flitted across Marsha's eyes. "That's a nice idea, Josie. Ask him, why don't you?"

"I will." I stood and yawned, stretching till my ribs cracked. "Have to go upstairs now. Still got a little left to do before school tomorrow. Maybe I'll talk to Dad when he comes in."

"Good enough," she said. Then, as if she'd changed her mind, "Maybe wait until morning; he's pretty tired tonight."

I nodded, smiling. She was funny. He was exhausted every night, but she wouldn't say that, because it sounded like a complaint. And, if he heard her, he might think she was unhappy because he's so much older than her. Twelve years. Dad is thirty-nine.

It was almost midnight when I finally closed my

notebook. As usual, lit took longer than I'd expected. Scrunched under the too-small, white student desk, my legs were cramping, and my eyes each had little bonfires blazing behind them. I packed up my books so I wouldn't have to bother in the morning, set the radio-alarm, slipped off my jeans, and crawled into bed still wearing my bra, "Poison" sweatshirt, and panties.

Sometime later — maybe minutes, maybe hours — the door downstairs creaked open, then closed again. With a metallic grunt, the deadbolt turned. I didn't actually hear all this, but I knew somewhere in the back of my brain what was going on. A minute later I felt the light vibration of steps crossing my room. A creepy prickle danced up my spine, and I knew somebody was watching me while I slept. But I couldn't open my eyes. Then something warm whisked over my forehead.

"Good-night, Josephine," whispered a disembodied voice.

I thought the words: Good-night, Daddy.

"Now, don't quit yet! Three more sets, and . . . one, two, three, four . . ."

Marsha was evidently well into "20-Minute Work-out" downstairs. Throwing back the blankets, I shivered my way across the hall to the bathroom. I showered with super-hot water, blew my hair dry, dressed and was headed for an English muffin when I heard a soft sound, not quite what you'd classify as human.

"Chriss-eeee!" I moaned, shaking my head. "All right. I'm coming."

Marsha would be ticked off that he'd waked up early. She liked to jog two miles after her warm-up. Usually she made it back and had time to shower before Chrissy either bellowed the house down or engineered his own escape from the crib.

I headed straight into his room, then stopped dead.

There he was, knotted up like a puppy in his blanket, one finger coiled in a strawberry-red tendril near his ear. His little face was totally relaxed, except for his pouty mouth that worked in gentle sucking motions. Chrissy was zonked out cold.

I turned away, confused, then almost immediately heard it again: a sharp, high-pitched intake of breath, like a pitiful gasp from a cornered guinea pig. Only we don't have a guinea pig.

I stared at my parents' door, directly across the hall. It was closed; no light shone from underneath.

"And, keep it up! Bounce, two . . . bounce, three . . . bou-ou-ounce, four . . ." The inane TV voice blared from the living room.

I took two steps into the hall, shutting Chrissy's door behind me. "Dad?" I called softly. After another minute I raised my hand and knocked. No answer.

"Daddy?" I slowly opened his door.

He wore a bright red tartan robe and lay on his back, pajamaed shins crossed. His hands were wedged behind his wide neck, and he stared intently at the ceiling.

"You all right?" I asked, stepping closer.

There was a minute before his gaze shifted. At first he seemed startled, as if he didn't recognize me, then his gray eyes softened. "Off to school, are we?"

"Yes."

"Have a good day, then." And he smiled, but not in his usual carefree way. His mouth just sort of twisted into a crooked shape with no other part of his face responding.

I moved closer, then hesitated. I wanted to ask him why he'd been gone so long the night before. But maybe that was none of my business.

I looked around the room. His clothes were tossed in a pile on the floor; the tips of his tan Hush Puppies peeked out from underneath.

I said, "I heard a funny sound. Like a cry. Are you all right?"

"Fine." He blinked at me, as if surprised I should ask. "Great." Dad sat up a bit and slid his own plus Marsha's pillows under his head, thumping them with his fists. "Just taking the day off." He reached over and tapped the morning newspaper, which lay on the rumpled sheets next to him. "Going to take it easy," he explained. "Going to play hooky for once."

"Sure." I nodded, as if this made perfect sense when you considered unexplained whimpers and him disappearing for half the night. "Well, you certainly deserve it."

"Yes," he said. But he sounded as if he was trying to convince himself, and he avoided my eyes. "I'll sell two houses tomorrow, to make up for the one I might have missed today."

I stared at him for a few seconds, then bent down and planted a kiss right on the tip of his nose, like always. "Good for you," I murmured. After all, he was perfectly justified in staying up late or taking a day off. It wasn't as if he needed my permission or anything. And I didn't like to think of myself as nosy. "See you after school," I told him, and turned to leave.

"Right. Possibly . . ."

I circled back. He was blinking into space, and I realized for the first time how red and flaky with fatigue his eyes were.

"Possibly," he began again, "we can do something together . . . when you get home, Josephine."

"What about Riveredge?" I asked impulsively.

He blinked once more, at last glancing directly up at me. His arms and legs seemed suddenly rigid. "You still interested in shooting?"

I bobbed my head up and down vigorously. "I've been going at least once a week. Brian, too."

"Don't you work tonight, Josephine?"

"There're still a couple of hours after school before I have to be at Harvey's. All three of us can drive up." I grinned encouragingly. "It'll be fun. Honest. You can give Bri some pointers. And," I joked, "*I'll* give *you* some."

He was observing his hands, running one thumbnail under those of the other hand, as if cleaning them. From where I stood, they looked spotless.

"I didn't realize you were still into that sort of thing," Dad grumbled. "Still have that gun?"

I looked at him really hard now, unable to see what he was getting at. "Yeah."

"We should get rid of it. Dangerous for a kid. Dangerous for anyone."

I don't often explode. I sort of pride myself on having outgrown temper tantrums about the time my first mother walked out on me and Dad. I was five years old then. I'd hurt so bad inside, but I wouldn't let myself cry. I guess I figured listening to me bawling would make Dad feel even worse. Or maybe I was secretly afraid that if I carried on and was too much trouble — well, Dad might take off, too.

But now my mouth dropped open in shock, and I yelled, "My Browning Citori! *You* gave it to me. You

16

gave it to me for my tenth birthday!"

He bit his lower lip and flinched as if startled by how loud I was talking all of a sudden. "We all make mistakes," he said at last. "There's a lot to be said for gun control. You read every day about violence in some household, accidental deaths that wouldn't have happened if a gun hadn't been there."

"But that's different," I gasped. "Those people are messing around with weapons they know nothing about. You taught me how to handle a gun. I'm always careful. You know that."

"Christopher is getting older," he continued as if he hadn't heard me. "He's into everything now."

Which was true. However, the Citori was kept locked in a special cabinet in the den. It was the only gun we had now, since Dad had sold his Remington a year ago, saying he intended to replace it with something heavier. Only he hadn't.

"Chrissy can't get into the gun cabinet," I objected, trying to sound reasonable and make the words come out one at a time instead of in excited glumps. "And, when he gets old enough, you'll want to teach him to shoot, too."

"Kids your age get all sorts of wild ideas," he whispered, sounding morose.

"Dad!"

He narrowed his eyes at me. "Brian. Is he pushing this shooting business? Why is he all of a sudden so hot on guns? Boys think they're macho if they tote a gun around."

My hands, already tight at my sides, clenched into balls. And I felt myself start to shake with the unfairness of what I was hearing.

"What are you saying, Dad? Listen to yourself. Brian is a very responsible person. You make him sound like a street-gang punk!"

He turned his head slightly against the pillowcase and focused on the ceiling. His voice dropped off to a hoarse, expressionless whisper. "Sell the gun, Josephine, if you want money for it. Otherwise, I'll trash it."

"Fine. Well, that's just fine," I sputtered, backing out the door. "Give me a present, then take it away!"

Downstairs the TV was silent. Marsha had gone jogging. In the kitchen I found the English muffin I'd planned on for breakfast, still in the freezer, frozen solid. I grabbed my books and left.

# CHAPTER THREE

THE QUESTION SAID:

> "Everyone suspects himself of at least one of the cardinal virtues, and this is mine: I am one of the few honest people that I have ever known." Identify the author and the cited work.

I lifted my head and glanced across the packed classroom. Mary Chang, her smooth black hair slick against one plump cheekbone, was still writing like mad. I rolled my eyes back to the test paper and bit off the rubber nub of my eraser pen.

First period, Mr. Perry had given a pop quiz in Algebra II. The equations weren't very involved, but I couldn't seem to remember how to find a common denominator. That had screwed up half my answers. The rest of the day had gone downhill from there.

By seventh we were having a test in lit, the subject in which I usually did best. But my brain was still hanging halfway between home and a multiple variable, in no way distinguished by any cardinal virtue I could think of.

I kept seeing my father, stretched out stiffly on his bed in his red robe, red eyes — lying to me. I knew him well enough to know that all that drivel about taking a spontaneous day off was something he'd made up to put me off. He's just too organized a person. I mean, here is a man who coordinates (down to his socks and cuff links) what he'll be wearing the next day before he goes to bed at night; who has the lawn mower overhauled every fall so it'll be all ready for the next spring; who has his Christmas shopping finished in August, for crying out loud! And, almost as bad as shutting me out, he was cutting down everything I cared about — my shooting, his gift to me, Brian. My stomach tightened into a small hard knot. I just couldn't think straight.

"Scott Fitzgerald," I plucked out of the air, and scribbled his name before I could change my mind a fourth time. Last week we'd finished *The Great Gatsby*. Good old F. Scott was Mrs. Horndiker's pet writer, so she'd be sure to stuff plenty of his quotes into the test. Odds were in my favor.

I filled in most of the other blanks, then scrawled my name across the head of the top sheet and passed it in as soon as the bell rang. Half the class was still writing.

"Take your time!" sang out Horndiker, as if she was inviting everyone to stay for a second piece of apple pie.

I made straight for my locker and started pulling out

19

books like crazy. They thudded into a heap on the linoleum. More doors flew open, and the corridor was suddenly crammed with bodies and filling up with noise.

Two guys in black-and-red warm-up jackets brushed by. "Hey! I'm impressed!" Craig Bush shouted so everybody could hear when he saw me heft the entire stack. Marty Ford, matching Craig's six feet three inches but slimmer, smiled dimly, as if he wished he'd thought of that gem.

"Get lost," I growled. I'd probably bombed two tests in one day. Two! And in subjects where I never got less than a B.

It was all Dad's fault. Why was he acting so spacey? I mean, when you depend on someone your whole life, you get used to them being a certain way. If they start acting the exact opposite, it's bound to shake you up. I had no patience that day for Craig and Marty.

"Tetchy, tetchy," scolded Craig, shaking a finger wide as a broom handle.

I kicked the locker shut, a ton of books wobbling in my arms, and started down the hall. I couldn't remember what subjects I had assignments in. If I took everything home, maybe my head would clear. Or, I could call somebody later and sort this all out. With midterms coming up, I couldn't afford to have too many days like this.

At the end of the hall I ran into Mary.

"Why didn't you wait?" she asked. Her cheeks glowed pink and she was out of breath, although she'd only run a couple dozen feet.

"Do you have to write a damn book every time you take a Horndiker test?" I grumbled, still walking. "You'll make us both miss the bus."

"Ooh!" Her brows rose in question. "Still bit-chy, are we? What's wrong, Josie?"

"You don't talk like that in front of your parents," I snapped, without thinking much about what was coming out of my mouth. "Why do you do it in school? Expect someone to be" — Craig's word came to mind — "impressed?"

Her mouth slackened, and her chin dropped. Her glittery black eyes drew together.

"You don't have to wait," she said softly. "It's okay."

She turned and walked off toward the math wing. I watched for a few seconds; her shoulders were quivering. She was probably bawling.

"Wonderful!" I muttered, and started after her. Biting off Craig's head was one thing. I doubted if the worst insult could penetrate that mule brain. But Mary, I knew, meant well enough. She wasn't the sort to pry or tease when you were feeling down. And if you got irritated with her, she always blamed herself — even if she hadn't done anything wrong.

She was leaning against her locker but hadn't opened it. Her eyes appeared to be dry. "It's not you," I whispered. "I didn't mean all that."

"You're r-r-right." She stammered slightly, so I knew she'd been really fighting the tears. There were still a lot of people in the halls, hurrying to make the buses or get to after-school activities. She'd be embarrassed if they saw her crying. "I like to say stuff I know would shock my parents, but only when they're not around. I'm false."

I laughed and shook my head, then hugged her. She has a sort of formal and offbeat way of expressing herself sometimes. When she talks in clichés, she al-

21

ways mixes them up. But she just doesn't know any better. Her mother is Filipino and her father Chinese. They are quiet, terribly dignified people; speak four languages (at last count), and have rice paper shades over light bulbs for lamps. Mrs. Chang teaches watercolor-painting classes nights at the YMCA. Mr. Chang is a chemist for Pfizer, the pharmaceutical company in town.

I said quietly, "It doesn't hurt anyone."

She sighed once more and stared at me, hard, concentrating on keeping back the flood.

"Come on, get your stuff," I told her, and dialed her combination. "We'll both miss the bus."

The driver glared daggers at us as we squeezed down the aisle between people's knees. There weren't two seats together, and the bus started moving before either of us found a place.

At our stop on Tyler, I got out and waited at the bottom of the steps for Mary. Her house is directly behind ours.

"It's Brian," I said before she had a chance to speak.

Her face immediately cleared, and she almost smiled before remembering that, under the circumstances, she shouldn't be looking too deliriously cheery. "I'm sorry, Josie. What's wrong?"

The books were getting heavy; I shifted them so the edges would cut off the circulation a couple inches higher up on my arms. "My dad is all uptight about him."

"Why?"

"He says it's because of Riveredge. Doesn't want me shooting anymore, and thinks Brian's obsessed with guns or something. I don't know." I shrugged. "I don't

22

believe him. I don't think that's what is really bothering him."

"Why not?"

"It's just not like him to order me around this way." I glanced at her face. She was trying to look sympathetic, but it was obvious she didn't understand any more than I did. I decided to change the subject. "Do you work tonight?"

We'd both gotten jobs at Harvey's last summer. It was the first time either of us had worked, and applying together made it easier, more like joining a club. But we both wanted pocket money of our own, so we'd feel more independent and be able to afford a few luxury items, now and then, like a record album or extra-nice clothes or tickets to a rock concert in Hartford. It had worked out pretty well.

"No," she said. "I'm off. You?"

"Sanville has me scheduled for tonight, Thursday, and Friday. But I'm asking for Friday off."

"Because of Michelle's party?"

"Umm." I looked sideways at her solemn, dark eyes under a fringe of ebony bangs, wanting to be diplomatic after putting her down once already that day. "I don't suppose it will be a very good party . . . not really. So you won't be missing much if you can't come."

She grinned, then squeaked excitedly. "But, for once, I can come! My mother called Mrs. Vonnegut and rolled out the law: no booze, no lights out, and an adult in the room at all times."

Laid down the law, I thought. That's what she means. I laughed. "You're kidding! Your quiet little mother tackled the president of the League of Women Voters and *told* her how to run her daughter's party?"

23

Mary looked extremely serious. "She honestly did, Josie. I was so mortified. But" — she brightened considerably as we came to a stop near her father's forsythia bushes — "Michelle's mother said she agreed totally and made her feel so confident about the party, I'm allowed to go."

"That's great!" Sounded like a dud of a party, actually. But I didn't say so. Mary's parents didn't let her go out much.

She lowered her lashes briefly and blushed before stammering. "Do you th-think Martin will be there?"

"Boy, you sure pick 'em," I teased, nudging her in the ribs with my elbow. "Think you can handle a jock like that?" Marty Ford didn't seem at all her type. Intellectually he was on a par with a mushroom.

She smiled softly. "I think he's nice, under all that padding and . . . whatever it is they wear for the football games."

I almost choked, remembering the broad, muscled shoulders and thighs Marty had developed over the summer. Sure, I thought, nice.

"Well, good luck," I told her, and we separated to go to our own houses.

As I tramped the last few yards toward my own back door, the amused smile Mary always managed to leave me with slowly faded. I drew a deep breath.

Talking to Mary had calmed me down some. But now that I was alone and home, the tension began to claw at my stomach again. I sensed that everything Brian and I had together was in jeopardy.

Cautiously, I let myself in the back door with my key. "Anyone home?" I called up the stairs.

Nothing.

"Dad?" There was still no answer. I felt better.

*　*　*

FOR A TUESDAY NIGHT HARVEY'S HAMBURGERS WAS busy. There were five waitresses. Gus, a skinny black guy who'd graduated last year, was on the grill. And Sanville even scuttled out of his office to take over the register when people wanting to pay their checks lined up and blocked customers who were waiting for booths.

I had the last six booths, which are always full, no matter what. Between taking orders and wiping tables, I cornered Sanville and got permission to skip Friday. He wasn't happy about it though. I felt as if I was selling my soul, but whatever I had to do later to make up for the free night, I figured was worth it. He switched me over to Saturday. And next time he was short a girl, I'd be the first one he'd call. Which meant, at the very least, another set of back-to-back nights. Maybe even three in a row.

We closed at ten. When I pulled Marsha's car into the drive behind the Seville I sat there, watching the front windows for a few minutes. My room was dark, and so was Chrissy's. The lights were still on in the living room, though, and no one had drawn the drapes.

Against the artificial glare, I could see Dad sitting in his favorite Naugahyde recliner. But the chair wasn't in its usual position — back to the kitchen and facing the living room picture window. He'd pushed it into the narrow corner between the window and end wall, leaving no space at all behind. And he seemed to be watching the front door.

We hadn't seen each other since I'd stormed out of the house that morning. I'd been so furious with him, and I knew I still wouldn't be able to make him understand why. My gut rumbled nervously. My mouth tasted dry. What if he was waiting up for me? What

25

if I walked in and the first thing he said was: "I don't want you seeing that gunslinger Brian Pedersen anymore."

I ran my palms around the bumpy steering wheel, feeling the plastic cool down with the motor off. My breath was fogging the windshield.

But I couldn't very well sit out there all night. "It's my house, too," I muttered, yanking the keys out of the ignition and grabbing my purse.

Between the driveway and the front door I crammed down a lungful of air. My fingers tightened around the denim strap of my purse. I told myself, "This is ridiculous. You don't even know why you're afraid of him. Words. All he can do is say something you don't want to hear. But you can talk him out of it, Josie, if you stay cool."

He must have been asleep, I realized as I stepped inside. At the sound of the latch, his lids flew open wide. And his hand slipped from his lap to the cushion next to his hip. Something gleamed between his fingers. A glass, I guessed at first, he's afraid of spilling something. But almost immediately I knew I was wrong. Whatever he was hiding was way too small for any kind of cup or glass, and it caught the light like dulled metal.

"Hi," I chirped mechanically, raising a hand.

His eyes settled on me. For an instant they softened, but then flashed around the rest of the room, and beyond, into the dining room and kitchen, parts of which were visible from the new position of his chair. He glared suspiciously at every dark corner. He looked to be in a terrible mood.

I started to say something, but changed my mind. We Monroes always talk things out. Dad used to tease me about a zero generation gap in our house. But now all I could think about was the way he'd acted that morning. It made me angry all over again, and I decided I didn't particularly want to chat. In fact, it would probably be wiser *not* to start a discussion right now.

"Going straight to bed?" he asked when I took a few steps toward the stairs. He looked a little sad.

I nodded.

In my room, I shut the door quietly and sat on the edge of my bed. Kicking off my Red Cross waitressing shoes, I pulled the spiderweb net off my pinned-up hair. But until I heard him come upstairs and go into his room, I don't think I really breathed.

After a while I felt less jittery and figured I'd be able to fall asleep faster if I filled the hollow place in my stomach first.

Downstairs was totally dark, except for the light Marsha always left on over the stove. I padded across the cold linoleum and checked out the fridge: two slices of old carrot cake, and orange Jell-O that had been left uncovered and was going stiff. The rest was condiments and the sacks of white and wheat flour and cornmeal Marsha stored there so the meal worms wouldn't get into them.

A gallon milk jug had about an inch left at the bottom. I settled for that, with six spoonfuls of Ovaltine. I didn't even run it through the blender to froth it up; I didn't want anyone coming down.

# CHAPTER FOUR

I INTENDED TO REGISTER A FORMAL COMPLAINT. BEFORE I'd left for Harvey's last night, supper had been just me, Chrissy, Marsha (Dad, apparently, didn't show up until after I'd left), and a pot of chicken rice soup. The soup had been okay, but it hadn't stayed with me through a night of shuffling plates. And when I'd sneaked back down to the kitchen later that night, the refrigerator had been picked pretty well bare. Which is really strange.

Marsha, you see, for all her fitness hang-ups, is one of the best all-time junk-food middlemen around. In fact, for the first six months of my freshman year, I was so spaced out by high school that I went on a Twinkie binge. (Some people drink or smoke pot when they're depressed. I do Twinkies.) Without batting an eye she'd kept me in fine supply.

I don't think I'm spoiled. I'd have done the same for her. At certain times of the month, she gets sugar cravings, and I smuggle her bulk dark chocolate from Viccelli's Candies next door to Harvey's. She'd really disappointed me this time.

That morning Chrissy came into my room while I was dressing. He stood watching while I pulled my slip down over my head. "What you think you are?" he scolded in his baby voice. "A pwin-cess?"

My hair was still stuck up on my head from last night. Sanford makes all the girls wear a hairnet, which looks tacky with long hair. Most of us pin it up first. And the white nylon slip clung to me at the right curves and flat places like a gown, so I could see why Chrissy thought I looked dressed up.

I laughed and tugged out bobby pins, tossing them on the dresser.

"No," I said, then spun on him. I lunged, scooping his chunky, corduroyed body to my hip. I told him, "I am Cleopatra! My asp is after — *you!*" I snapped at his rotund belly with a puppet-shaped hand. He squealed and wriggled in my arms. I kept it up until tiny tears spilled from his bright blue eyes.

"More — more — " he gasped when I put him down.

"You're a masochist, Christopher. Listen, how did you get out of bed so early?"

He beamed. "Chrissy climb."

"Oh, swell." I mussed his orange curls. "Marsha must be thrilled." The crib was her last respite. So long as he stayed in it, she could have an hour to herself, morning and afternoon, while he napped. No telling what a taste of freedom would do for him.

I changed my mind about what to wear, took off the slip, and pulled on an oxford shirt, oversize sweater of neon green cotton, and jeans. I just felt in too much of a rush to bother with a skirt.

In the back of my mind was a goal. I wanted to leave the house before Dad got up. And I was sure he hadn't because I'd have heard the shower or his electric razor running. The way he'd been acting was just making me too edgy. I didn't want to start off another day with a fight; I just couldn't afford to mess up on too many tests in my junior year. This year's grades would be sent to colleges, and I wanted them to look good.

Chrissy sat on my bed playing with my lipsticks and eyeliners while I finished dressing. Then, balancing books in one arm, I held his fat fingers with my free hand and we went down together.

About the third stair from the bottom, I realized Marsha was in the kitchen. I could hear her running water in the sink, opening and closing the dishwasher.

"Well?" said a deep voice. Dad.

I paused on the step, listening; Chrissy scowled up at me because I'd stopped.

"Well, *what*?" she returned, her voice tight.

"What are you going to do about it?"

I poked my head around the corner. Dad was seated at the kitchen table, a cup of black coffee in front of him.

"You have a young child who needs milk regularly," he went on. "Don't you think you'd better get your act together?"

She said nothing at first, then it was as if she was measuring out each word in one even tone. "You're-just-irritated-because-you-don't-have-milk-for-your-coffee."

"That, too. It'd be nice to have a tablespoonful, seeing as how coffee's my entire breakfast."

I coughed tactfully and entered the battleground. I didn't want to; there just didn't seem to be much else I could do, considering I had Chrissy. And, besides, I was going to have to get past them to get out the door. Sliding Chrissy into his high chair, I locked the tray over his tummy.

Marsha looked at me with a wounded, loser's expression. I should have taken some of the heat off her by confessing I was the culprit who'd used up the last of the milk. But I sort of thought she had it coming. I would have told her I didn't appreciate a foodless kitchen, if Dad hadn't beat me to it. I just didn't like the way he was doing it. He was being awfully mean.

So, I judiciously refrained from asking what was for breakfast. After scrounging around, I found that even the English muffin I'd seen the day before was gone. But there was a quarter loaf of white bread jammed into the back of the freezer and some room-temperature margarine in a plastic tub on the table. I stuck four slices into the toaster.

"Want toast, Christopher?" I asked with an inviting grin. As if gourmets flock from around the world to Chez Monroe for a nibble of this crunchy ambrosia.

"Mine!" he demanded with typical three-year-old possessiveness.

I buttered one slice and laid it on his tray.

Dad and Marsha exchanged looks, then she turned away to the side of the double sink where she was washing dishes. He stirred his cup of black coffee, and stared into it. I could feel the tension zinging between them across the room. My fingers felt numb as I tore my own toast in half. The stuff tasted like sponge rubber. But I made myself swallow.

At last Dad stood up from the table, walked over to the empty half of the sink in absolute silence, and poured the whole cupful of coffee down the drain in front of Marsha.

She stiffened, the heels of her hands pressing against the edge of the countertop.

"Get some damn milk today," he ordered coldly.

This is insane! I thought. Who in their right mind argues about milk?

"I have extra time before school," I said, trying to sound casual about it while munching my toast. "I'll pick it up — and anything else we need." He was badgering her, and that wasn't fair.

"No," Dad said. "Your mother is responsible for keeping this house in working order. She'll get the milk."

"I can't," she said rigidly.

"Why?" he roared.

31

"Because," she answered in a quiet voice, "I don't have any money. Give me some money, and I'll be glad to buy milk."

He turned pale, and his eyes slid away from her outstretched hand. Trudging out of the room, he kept going straight out the front door.

Marsha didn't move; suds dripped off her fingertips onto the floor.

"What's going on?" I asked.

Marsha shrugged, her eyes looking glazed.

"I'll pick up some milk at the Seven-Eleven. I have at least enough change in my jacket pocket for a quart." She didn't seem to hear me. "I said, I'll — "

"No," she whispered. "That's all right, Josie. You'd better go along to the bus stop; you'll be late for school. Don't worry about it."

I DIDN'T ACTUALLY WORRY ABOUT IT, BUT I COULDN'T stop replaying our cheery family breakfast scene throughout the day. On the way home I got off the bus two stops early. As I walked into the convenience store, I saw two seniors at the video games. They couldn't have beat me there; they looked too at ease, as if they'd been there for hours.

For some reason, I thought of Brian. He'd never cut classes to hang out like that. Then I thought of Dad and Marsha. And suddenly the whole business about the milk seemed comical. I could imagine Marsha already having shopped for milk and lots of other things like chips and soda and bologna and fresh bread. Maybe Dad had, too. And now I would. We'd all three wind up at home with milk, milk, and more milk. And we'd laugh at each other.

It was all a misunderstanding.

I picked up a couple of Twinkies on the way to the register, then went back for a small loaf of wheat bread. It would keep fine in the freezer if we suddenly had too much. And I couldn't survive without toast in the morning.

Out in the parking lot, I waited while two cars backed around and drove off into the street. The lot was too small for the business the store did. Several cars always had to park across the street.

It was less than a mile home. I'd cross farther down, then work my way along the next two blocks before cutting through yards.

I was halfway across the parking lot when the explosion shook the glass panes along the front of the store.

I jumped, letting loose a shriek, and juggled the brown paper sack. Two more sharp pops followed from very near. Other people around me jerked their heads this way and that, trying to locate the source of the earsplitting noise. I suppose they were thinking — gunshots. But I knew the difference; it was only the suddenness and the loudness that had startled me.

A rusty VW putt-putted backward in a semicircle, then, letting off two more volleys, wheezed on down the road. A sort of ordered calm was restored. People began moving again, laughing nervously at themselves. Then I spotted the crowd.

People were standing in the middle of the street, looking down at the ground. One woman was stooping, as if she was speaking to someone lying on the pavement. There must have been an accident, someone hit by a car.

A man in a sport coat broke away from the group and began directing traffic, like a cop, waving vehicles down with two hands over his head, then drawing a circle in the air to make them go around the gathering crowd.

I couldn't see the injured person or any blood on the road, but I didn't really want to go closer to investigate. The idea of someone being in pain while others stood around gawking disgusted me. Besides, I thought, there's nothing I can do; someone will have called an ambulance by now.

I walked on, skirting the crowd. Then the knot suddenly loosened as a few people drifted off, and the man on the ground became visible.

Brown hair was nearly covered by arms thrown up over his head in a protective gesture, and long legs in tan slacks were tucked up under his hips. He reminded me of a tortoise, head and feet pulled into its shell. His whole body rocked rhythmically from the knees.

I froze, and a slow sourness eased into my midsection. Something was very wrong here, more wrong than an ordinary, nasty hit-and-run accident.

Then my glance fell to the man's shoes. The suede Hush Puppies looked familiar. I studied them closely, and horror swept over me.

"Daddy!" I screamed. Dropping my books and the bag of groceries, I ran toward him.

# CHAPTER FIVE

"I'M A NURSE," SAID THE WOMAN WHO WAS STOOPING beside my father.

"What's wrong with him?" I put my hand on his shoulder. He jumped as if it'd given him an electric shock, then he stayed very still.

34

"Dad?" I cried in his ear. "What happened? Where are you hurt?"

He didn't answer, but the side of his neck near his wrist drew into a tight blue cord. Something wet covered the pavement and seeped through the knees of my jeans. It was chalky white, though, not red. I saw a split-open Dairy Dew carton lying next to him. Milk, I thought vaguely. He got the dumb milk, too.

Frantically, I inspected his legs, his back, his head — what I could see of it between his arms. All I found was a little scrape beneath one ear.

"I don't think it's anything serious," said the woman. She had almost white hair and a young face with kind eyes.

I glared at her and demanded, "Then why doesn't he get up?" I couldn't believe anyone could be so stupid.

She glanced up at the others still standing above us, as if to consult them. A man in trucker's overalls rolled his eyes. A woman in a business suit looked flustered and immediately walked away.

The nurse was patting my back and talking softly. "An ambulance will be here any minute, hon. Why don't you just wait; the medics will help your father."

Confused and feeling helpless, I swallowed the tears running down the back of my throat. After a minute, when I could trust my voice, I leaned over him and whispered. "It's me — Josie. Everything's all right. Somebody called for an ambulance."

Dad pulled away from me and lowered his arms, digging his fingers into the solid, flat tar of the road as if he could get a grip on it. And he rotated his head slightly to stare at me.

"No!" He was shaking, and his voice was sharp and

35

dry. "Tell them to go away. Tell them to leave me the hell alone."

I started crying for real now. "What's wrong with you?"

"Poor kid," someone from the circle muttered.

A siren was moaning, getting louder and louder.

Then a man's voice said in a confidential tone. "Damn shame. Little girl having an old man like that."

"High as a kite," said another with a chuckle.

I glared up at them. They each gave me a blank look, then turned and moved away. I bit my lip. My face felt hot and I wasn't so scared now, just mad. Mad at these ignorant people who stood around and did nothing but say cruel things when somebody was hurt.

Jerks! I thought.

"Come on, Dad." I could understand why he wanted to get away from these people. I put an arm under his shoulder and pulled up on it. "Let's get out of here."

"Yes," he said, and he staggered to his feet, looking dazed and leaning on me hard but moving along with purpose.

His car was across the street. I fished keys out of his pocket and let him in on the passenger side, then I ran back and picked up my books. Someone had swiped the bag of groceries, or maybe the stuff had slopped all over and been ruined anyway. I drove.

"We'd better go straight to the clinic," I said. "You should have X rays in case you've broken anything."

His head was down in his hands, and he didn't look at me. He seemed to be having trouble breathing. "No," he whispered. "I just want to go home."

I didn't argue. Marsha would know what to do. She'd make him see a doctor.

When we came through the front door Marsha was

in the kitchen with Chrissy, holding a knifeful of peanut butter in one hand. Her mouth fell a little bit open and she watched, not saying a word, while my father unsteadily climbed the stairs to his bedroom. Then she closed her lips and picked up a piece of bread and started spreading, making the strokes of the knife swirl the brown goo, round and round.

"What happened, Josie?" she asked at last, without glancing up.

I don't know exactly what I'd expected from her. But this wasn't it.

"He fell," I said. Maybe she was trying to stay calm so Chrissy wouldn't get scared. I tried to do the same. "Outside the Seven-Eleven. I think he must've hit his head. There's a cut."

She nodded, folded the bread in half, and gave it to Chrissy. He opened it up again and started eating the nuts out, one by one. There was peanut butter in his nose, on his chin and one ear.

"What are you going to do?" I asked, getting impatient. Soon someone would explain, then all this would make perfect sense. Like the M&M's puzzle that took us five weeks to piece together.

Marsha washed her hands in the sink, and wiped them carefully on a striped cloth hanging inside the cupboard. "I'll go up and check that scratch." She smiled from one corner of her lips. "I don't think it looked too bad. Do you?"

"You don't get the picture at all," I complained. And I blurted out everything that had happened. Except the stuff the jerks who'd stood around said, because I knew that would upset her.

"But he wouldn't stand up," I told her firmly. "He just stayed on the ground . . . and people stood there."

37

I looked her in the eyes. "Is he sick, is he dying or something?"

Marsha's glance shifted quickly away from mine. "Nothing like that, Josie. He was probably just stunned or something."

The phone rang. She trotted up the stairs instead of answering it. And I answered it instead of following her — which was what I really wanted to do.

"What's up, sexy?" It was Brian.

I carried the receiver across the kitchen and stared up toward the second floor. My parents' door was closed. I could hear voices but no words.

"Hi, Bri." I was dying to listen in on what was happening up there. I thought about how Marsha didn't seem at all surprised that her husband was falling down in the road and having to be driven home. And I thought about the trucker.

What if that idiot was right? I remembered how red Dad's eyes had been the morning before as he lay in bed. Then how he'd picked a fight over the milk. People who were heavy into alcohol looked like that and tended to start brawls for the littlest reasons. I'd seen it happen at a couple of parties. Some of the boys seemed to think it was funny to feed a friend more drinks than he could handle just to see how drunk and crazy he'd get. That always scared me, because sometimes the guy ended up driving home. And sometimes other people, who were either idiots or had been drinking too much themselves, got in the car with him.

Brian was saying something, but it didn't sink in. "I gotta go," I told him in desperation, and ran back across the kitchen to hang up.

As soon as I let go of the receiver, it flipped out of its metal sling and hit the floor with a crash. I spun

38

around. Chrissy had hold of the middle of the wire.

"Let go, you dumb kid!" I yelled at him.

He scowled and tightened his fist. Peanut butter oozed between his fingers and the corkscrewed cord.

"Crying out loud! Let go!"

With a long wail, he threw the wire away from him. He pounded his fists on the metal tray of his high chair, and the room sounded like the center of a thunderstorm.

I ran upstairs and met Marsha coming out of the bedroom. She shut the door behind her.

"Is he okay?" I asked, out of breath.

Marsha held a bottle of peroxide in one hand, a damp wad of cotton in the other. She walked past me into the bathroom. "Just fine," she said, sounding calm. After she tossed away the cotton and replaced the peroxide in the medicine cabinet, she turned around and looked at me closely. "That must have been difficult for you, Josie. I'm sorry you had to be there."

The clean, watery smell of the peroxide reminded me of all my own scraped knees and elbows that Dad had dabbed the stuff on.

"Someone had to help him," I said. "No one was doing anything."

She hugged me and stroked the back of my head. "You did just fine. It's scary when someone you love gets hurt."

"But he's all right now?"

"Yes." She sighed, pressing her cheek against my forehead. "He's fine. Don't worry, everything's — "

"Fine. I know," I grumbled. And if she said that word one more time, I was going to scream. Besides, people don't just collapse in the middle of a street for no reason. I didn't trust her, I decided. Maybe she *had* been nice to me, but she was keeping secrets. Dark, awful secrets, I was sure.

Marsha pulled away, suddenly alert. "What's that?"

A hiccuping whine rose from the kitchen. "That's your son," I said bitterly. "He's being a pain in the butt again."

She gave me a severe look and went downstairs.

After a few minutes I ran outside to get my books off the backseat of the car, then shut myself in my room. I wished I had the Twinkies now. I was unbelievably hungry.

The phone rang at four o'clock and Marsha shouted, "For you, Josie. It's Brian."

"Why'd you hang up on me?" he asked, sounding very worried.

I sat down at the kitchen table and made a point of crossing my heels on top of it.

Marsha didn't say a thing. She was still finding and wiping up little dabs of peanut butter on the floor, the high chair, and phone cord. I thought that if it turned out I was one of those women who could never have a baby, that might not be so bad.

"I didn't hang up on you," I explained. "I just had to do something, and it couldn't wait."

"Is anything wrong?"

"No," I lied. I wanted to be alone with him. I wanted to tell him everything and hear what he thought.

But I kept wondering — what if Dad's an alcoholic, or worse? What if he's into some sort of drug: PCP, or coke, or something? It wasn't just kids who got strung out on stuff. And, if he was, how could I ever face Brian? Your dad's a police officer. Mine is a junkie. Don't we make a nice pair? It had to be something bad, otherwise Marsha wouldn't be so hyper and secretive all at the same time!

"I don't work tonight," I said, switching subjects, not too deftly.

"I know, but I can't get the car."

"Oh." A sour, bubbly feeling was growing in my stomach. My hands felt cold and sweaty against the plastic thing pressed to my ear. I didn't like not getting problems out in the open.

"Look, Josie, if something's bothering you, you'd better tell me."

"Just lit." I was getting pretty good at lying, I thought regretfully. But I couldn't talk while Marsha hung around. "The test today was the pits. I think I bombed."

"And that's all?"

"Right," I said.

After I'd hung up, I walked out of the kitchen and up the stairs, turned left into the bathroom, then shut the door. Suddenly I was real glad I hadn't eaten since lunch. When I bent double over the toilet, there wasn't too much to come back up.

# CHAPTER SIX

I'D STARTED BY ARRANGING BOOKS ACCORDING TO subject, in small stacks around me on the bedroom floor. That way I could see exactly how much I had to do.

Four assignments were absolutely, positively due the next day. The rest could wait, I decided.

After Brian's call, and my trip to the bathroom, I

stretched out on my stomach and picked at the beige threads in the carpet until one pulled out. Closing my eyes, I thought about lying in the sand last summer, feeling the hot tan grains, sharp and tiny, between my fingers. And the smell of the salt water, especially at low tide, when the bladder kelp and periwinkles cling to the rocks on the breakwater, glistening blue black in the hot sun.

Brian had come over at least three days each week, when he didn't have to baby-sit for his sister and three brothers while his mom worked. We'd spend the whole time at the beach and usually not come home until after dark.

We'd always take a ratty old blanket to spread on the dry sand up near the stone wall. That way no one walking by could kick sand in our eyes. It was also easier to read there, because of the narrow piece of shade the wall made all afternoon. But mostly we'd lie beside each other, talking, his bare arm across my stomach. And, if I kept my eyes shut, the sun would turn the backs of my lids into warm, orange screens and I could make images across them.

Like — Brian and Josephine, alone on a desert island. We have no choice but to be together, so there's nothing wrong with anything we do. We never wear clothes, except if it gets too cold, which it rarely does. We make love on the warm, flat rocks where the waves spray over the edge. Our babies nap in the shelter of the granite cleft in the point. They have Bri's blue eyes and pale sun-bleached hair like mine. . . .

At the soft knock on the door, I murmured, "Come in," and sadly opened my eyes because the island had gone.

Marsha poked her head inside. "You were so busy,

you probably didn't hear me call you for dinner."

"No, I didn't." I sat up, feeling irritated that she'd spoiled my daydream.

She saw the books on the floor. "A busy night?"

"Very." It didn't have to be — the homework load wasn't particularly heavy — but then I didn't seem to be moving very quickly. Maybe it would be late before I finished. Maybe I wouldn't be able to finish at all. "Could I have dinner in my room, please? So I can work while I'm eating?" I asked.

I expected her to say something about how digestive systems function best under nonstressful conditions. If she did, I was going to tell her that it would be impossible to eat in the same room with them. Monroes don't keep secrets. At least I'd never thought they did.

Dad had once told me why my real mother left us. They'd been married young — right after high school. The draft was on then because of the Vietnam War. So, just a couple of months after their wedding, he'd had to leave her in Connecticut. I was born while he was in the army.

After he left the service, my mother wanted to move to New York City so that she could have a career as a clothing buyer for a glamorous department store like Bloomingdale's. But Dad didn't like the idea of my growing up in a big city. They disagreed about a lot of other things, too, that hadn't seemed so important before he went into the army. Finally, she got tired of arguing and walked out.

Much later, he'd also told me he loved Marsha and was going to ask her to marry him — before he even mentioned it to her. Because he'd confided in me so many times about important things, I'd gotten to expect him always to tell the truth. Now I didn't know what

43

to think of my father, and I refused to talk to him and Marsha as if everything was normal.

"I'll bring your plate up," Marsha said after a minute.

I nodded. "Thanks."

By ten-thirty I'd managed to get just forty-five degrees around the circle. The phone rang again. Someone clomped down the stairs to answer it, and a moment later, Dad called for me.

If it was Brian, I wouldn't know what to say. But I'd rather it was him anyway.

Downstairs, only one light was on. That was in the living room where Dad was sitting in his recliner. I ran through, blindly heading into the dark kitchen. I reached onto the countertop and felt around. Nothing. Scowling into the blackness, I gave my eyes a minute to adjust, then saw that the receiver had already been hung up. I stood there, looking at it, trying to figure out what had happened.

"Come in here, Josephine," Dad called quietly.

He was still in the recliner.

"Who was that?" I asked, walking closer. "I thought you called me down because someone was on the telephone."

The brass arc lamp spotlighted him in a pool of yellow. His eyes looked heavy, and the skin around the red scrape below his ear stood out white and neat.

"That was the Pedersen boy."

I frowned, watching him through narrowed eyes. "What did you say to him?"

"Josephine," he began, "sit down. Let's talk."

The back of my neck prickled; I was instantly suspicious. "What did you tell Brian? Did you say I couldn't speak to him?"

"That boy," he said very slowly, "he's got no respect for privacy. He shouldn't be calling at this late hour. And besides, you've been talking to him all night."

Do you believe this? I thought. "I have not, Dad. I've been working in my room."

"How many times has he called?"

"Twice, before this. But the first time I — "

"If you're still doing homework at nearly eleven o'clock, it's because you're distracted." His voice was shaking now. "If you spent less time on that boy — "

I couldn't keep from shouting. "That's *not* why I'm distracted!"

He stood up abruptly and glared out the front window, putting his back to me.

Marsha came downstairs. She'd obviously been asleep and looked terrible. Her face was blotched and puffy from the pillow, little creases from the case puckering her cheeks. She blinked rapidly, as if trying to focus on what was going on.

"You're too young to be so serious with a boy," he continued, without turning around. "I think it's time we break this thing off."

"Break this *thing* off?" I sputtered. "You sound like you're amputating a tree limb!" I paced the floor between the sofa and recliner. "Brian doesn't call this late, usually. It's my fault. He thinks I'm mad at him." And that's all *your* fault, I added silently.

"He's simply causing too many problems in this family," Dad insisted. "You have no idea how dangerous a boy like that could be. You might get hurt."

"Dangerous?" I cried. "Brian?"

He turned to face me. His teeth were gritted, and his eyes were hard and cold. "You have to think about

45

your little brother, too. Think what Brian could do with a gun . . . to Chrissy."

My heart jumped up into my throat. I shook my head. "Dad, that's crazy. Brian would never — "

He cut me off. "I want you to stop seeing him."

"But I . . ." My comeback clogged in the back of my mouth as his words settled like a cold, winter fog around me, shutting out all love, all warmth. I swallowed. "He's my friend, the best one I have. And I — "

"Shut up!" he shouted, his voice cracking. "Just do what I tell you."

There isn't a whole lot of point in arguing anymore, I thought, looking away from his angry, determined eyes. He's made up his mind, and nothing I say or do right now is going to change it.

Still I couldn't help trying just once more. I glanced up from the floor, opening my mouth to speak, then I saw his fist. The veins stood out on the back of his moving hand.

I ducked backward as Marsha screamed, "Jack, no!"

His clenched fist jerked to a halt in midair, but the pulse points at his temples bulged with the effort of restraint.

Backpedaling, I tripped over Chrissy's Nerf ball and sprawled on the floor at Dad's feet.

He looked bewildered, as if he didn't know whether to be mad, afraid, shocked, or what. Tightening up once more, all over, he whipped around and slammed his knuckles against the wall next to the recliner. There was a barely noticeable pause while his hand burrowed into the wall, then a dull pop as the surface caved in, as if in slow motion, around his fist. White dust puffed out onto the carpet.

"What are you *doing?*" I heard myself scream hysterically.

Dad glared at me over his shoulder, as if the hole in the wall were my fault. I ran up to my room and locked the door behind me.

I don't think — no, I *know* I didn't sleep that night. I'd never been so scared in my life. Oh, sure, I was afraid of the usual stuff. Like getting killed in a car accident, or dying from some horrid disease while I was still pretty young — like Debra Winger in *Terms of Endearment*. But I'd never, *never* been afraid to be in the same house with my own family. And the way I felt now, I was thinking there wasn't anything worse.

Only, then, I didn't know that this was just the beginning.

## CHAPTER SEVEN

TRASH BARRELS STENCILED *STOW IT OR TOW IT* WERE lined up behind bleachers on the football field. I shrugged off my jacket, spread it on the ground, and sat down. The weather that day was unusually warm for November in Connecticut, and the ground hadn't frozen yet. After third period Mr. Renscheler, the assistant principal, had announced over the intercom that we could have lunch on the lower field.

The Townies were grouped in one end zone and someone had a box turned up loud enough to be heard in New York. A girl with spiked hair and a pink shirt that hurt your eyes when you looked at it was dancing. A guy sporting gold loops in his ears and a shadow of beard shouted obscene things at her good-naturedly.

"She must be a very strong-minded individual," remarked Mary, sounding wistful as she dropped a bag of corn chips in my lap and sat down cross-legged. She'd come down the long grassy slope behind the gym two minutes after me. I wondered if she knew how naive she sounded. "Doing just what you feel like when others disdain you," she added philosophically, "takes a lot of nerve."

"Or a lot of encouragement," I muttered. Fran Jeffers had already been suspended twice for smoking in the field behind the science wing — the wrong kind of cigarette.

"I think," said Mary after some thought, "she's probably lonely. You can tell; she just wants attention."

I tore open the cello bag between my teeth and watched the five or six guys who'd joined Fran's lone admirer. They were appreciating the way she bounced inside her shirt. "Well, I'd say she's going to get it."

Townies like Fran, I'd discovered, never quite know what to do with themselves. They're caught between the other two cliques at Groton.

Subbers — navy brats — make up almost half of the school. Most of their families are stationed in the area for only three years, so they register somewhere in the middle of high school, or else leave before they graduate. They're *very* serious, and the guys wear white dress shirts with the cuffs rolled and collars open, looking like junior accountants. The girls wear only the kind of jeans with a celebrity's name stitched on the backside, if they wear jeans at all. Usually they stick to preppy stuff, as though no one ever told them it's totally out now.

The Pointers live along the water. Their parents mostly are execs for General Dynamics, the shipbuilder that makes submarines for the Defense Department. Or else they're chemists for Pfizer, which makes pharmaceuticals. Of course, every doctor and lawyer in town lives on the point, too. We're there only because Dad's in realty and got a good deal on our house. Otherwise we'd have ended up downtown. Townies. And I don't think I'd have liked that.

Tori Wheeler, Carolyn Powers, and Michelle Vonnegut came over and sat down. They were deep into some discussion and nodded but didn't say anything in particular to us.

I thought it was strange; they didn't seem to be talking about Michelle's party. That sort of thing took a solid week or more of planning: Who was coming with whom. Who had broken up since the invitations had been sent out. What new pairs had formed in the last few days, which always meant extra, last-minute guests. The day before, I'd overheard Carolyn and Michelle discussing how to uninvite a particular sophomore. Carolyn "couldn't stand being in the same room with that little witch," and she was threatening not to come at all in order to avoid her. Since Carolyn and Michelle were best friends, the sophomore would somehow get dumped. It all got very complex, having a party.

Mary opened a napkin and spread it on her lap. She took a slender paring knife out of her purse, removed a plastic safety shield from the blade, and started peeling an orange. Carefully, she removed every trace of the white fiber without nicking the juicy pulp.

"Did you get back your French test?" she asked, her black eyes concentrating as she neatly separated the sections. "You were worried about it."

I munched the salty chips and sipped from the can

 Middlebury Public Library

of soda I'd bought from a machine in the cafeteria. "Got it," I said. "Didn't do bad. Could have been better, I guess. But I'm not complaining. How about yours?" I asked before she could demand anything more specific.

"You know vocab tests are always easy for me," she said matter-of-factly.

I laughed and shoved her with my elbow. "Just about everything is easy for you, Chang. I think the last time you didn't ace a test was when Frankel passed out the senior chem midterm by mistake."

"It isn't as easy as it looks," she said softly, then brightened. "But I did get a B on that test."

"You wily Orientals," I muttered. And we laughed. It was my standard dig at her.

We split her orange and lay back in the sun, licking our fingers. The football team was going around reminding people to use the trash cans. Which wasn't really necessary. Everyone knows that Renscheler personally checks the field after an outside lunch. We wouldn't get another one for the rest of the year if he found a mess. With that in mind, people generally pitched in, and those few that didn't got bad-mouthed by the rest.

It would have been a pretty nice day altogether, except for what was going on at home. I just couldn't shake the gloom. And what was I going to do about Brian?

"Got a couple of minutes?" a deep voice asked from behind us. Before I'd blinked once, Mary was on her feet and asking the tall guy with drowsy-looking eyes, "What time is it?"

I thought, if dogs actually do resemble their owners,

Martin Ford must have a basset hound.

"Twelve-thirty," he said, after consulting an enormous metal band on his wrist that looked as if it was capable of everything short of launching a space shuttle.

"Then we have fifteen minutes before last bell." Mary turned and explained, a flush creeping across her cheeks. "I volunteered to tutor during my free period, three days a week. We really need to set up a schedule. Do you mind, Josie?"

Her eyes were bright and wide and excited. I remembered when the volunteer forms had been passed out. She hadn't said anything about tutoring then. I figured she must have heard since then that Marty needed help in one subject or another.

"Go ahead," I told her, and smiled to show I meant it.

They strolled off, Marty putting his big, hard hand at the waist of her skirt. She looked up at him, for all the world as if he wore a cape and tights.

I knew she hadn't had much experience with boys. After all, we'd been friends since second grade and you don't keep that sort of information to yourself when you're that close.

I wasn't exactly scared for her. I supposed Marty might not be a bad guy. I didn't really know him. He was polite with her, the same way he acted with teachers and adults. But I wasn't sure what he'd be like on his own, and that worried me.

"Is your father better?" asked a voice close by.

Thoughts of Mary and Marty dissolved fast. "Huh?" I squinted into the autumn sun.

Michelle had slid over next to my jacket sleeve. Tori

and Carolyn were picking up their sandwich wrappings. I was sure they were listening, without wanting to look like they were.

"Your father," said Michelle in a sincere tone. "I heard he had . . . an accident."

"He's fine," I told her quickly, and felt suddenly chilled on the sunny field. My brain was clicking over a lot of possibilities. Where had she heard? How?

"I'm glad," she murmured. "My dad said it looked pretty serious."

I frowned. She couldn't possibly be saying what I thought she was saying. "He was there?" I couldn't imagine someone who knew me or my parents had walked off without trying to help. "I didn't see him," I continued warily.

"Oh." Michelle fluttered her pretty dark lashes. "I suppose he didn't want to interfere."

Or become involved, I thought bitterly. Like the rest of them there, thinking the worst — that he was drunk, or stoned crazy and on some sort of bad trip.

There was another ten minutes before lunch was over, but now it didn't seem worth hanging around. "Think I'll go on inside," I told them. "I've got some things to do."

"See you at the party . . . tomorrow night," Michelle called after me.

Tori and Carolyn were standing on either side of her when I looked back. Of course, they'd heard everything.

At one time, I'd been very close to Tori. She was a nice person. Very bubbly and into anything that involved being in the spotlight — cheerleading, drama club, prom committee — but she wouldn't spread malicious gossip like Carolyn or Michelle. I wondered why she hung out with them.

"You'll be there. Won't you, Josie?" Carolyn shouted when I didn't answer, a snicker underlying her voice.

"Yeah," I said, already having second thoughts. "Sure."

IN ALGEBRA, MR. PERRY SHOWED A FILM STRIP, THE OLD kind where someone has to turn the knob on the projector at the beep on a record. Everyone got giddy because it felt like first grade all over again. And when he had to leave the room to take a phone call, Kevin Treat, who was "cameraman," ran it on the ceiling. So we all hunkered down in our seats to be able to see, and the narrator's face looked pockmarked from the holes in the acoustical tile.

I laughed so hard my sides hurt. I laughed because I wanted to have something to laugh about more than anything else in the world. Something was bottled up inside me. I had to let it out.

When Perry came back and asked if the film had helped straighten out any confusion about inequalities, I'd gotten to the point where anything anybody said was hilarious.

I shut my mouth hard and tried to think of something grotesque and sobering, like a poor little sparrow run down in the road. But those moronic giggles kept sputtering out. Everyone else managed to keep a straight face. Tori flashed me a questioning look that said, Are you in your right mind? The strange thing was, laughing didn't make me feel any better. It just tightened me up worse inside.

"Miss Monroe," said Perry as the class filed past his desk after the bell.

He wore a brown polyester suit the same color as the ring of hair over his ears. He'd have made a great monk — Friar Perry, Robin Hood's right-hand man. I almost started again, then pulled my mouth back into line.

"I'm sorry," I said. "I hope I didn't disrupt the class. I seem to be in an odd mood."

"I'd say." He squared up a stack of papers on his desk. "And the homework assignment? I don't see yours among these."

"I'm a little backed up," I admitted. "May I have another day?"

He nodded and began shoving papers into his briefcase. He watched what he was doing, and not me. "Your test on Tuesday was far from your best effort, Josephine." Perry never calls students by their first names, and it made me nervous that he did now, to me. "While working on tonight's material, I'd review those back pages if I were you. They'll be included on the midterm exam."

I figured if I started working on the bus I could get the whole thing out of the way early. But when we lurched out of the parking lot, I thought about Brian again and never opened my notebook.

There'd been no way to call him since the night before; he'd been in school, too. And Michelle's party was only a little over twenty-four hours away. Although he'd said we could go, that was before everything that happened. We both knew I hadn't been straight with him the first time he called. And, later on, I suspected he'd gotten a lecture from my father. At least a lecture. Maybe he'd told Brian never to call again, never to come by the house or to see me.

I glowered out the bus window as the driver downshifted and we jounced to the bottom of Long Hill. The little barber shop and liquor store looked dismal and dirty under a solid gray sky that had rolled in around noon.

"Are you mad at me, Bri?" I whispered, and the glass fogged where my breath hit, blurring the buildings and trees. Even if I could patch things up between us before the next night, it'd be risky going to Michelle's house. If I told Dad that Brian wouldn't be there, he might find out anyway, then . . . I shut my eyes and tried not to imagine life without Brian.

Mary was staying after school. She hadn't said why, but that seemed pretty obvious. The football team had practice on Thursdays. Probably Marty had asked her to stay and watch. He'd be that way — want to show off. So, I was the only one to get off at the corner of Tyler. And I felt myself tensing, every step closer I got to the house.

No one was home though. Marsha had left a note saying she was at the library with Chrissy for story hour. I turned on the stereo and switched the AM dial to the only New York station that came in decent.

Nobody had bothered to cover up the hole in the living room wall. I found a rectangular piece of corrugated cardboard in the basement and taped it over the crumbling edges of wallboard. If anyone asked, I'd tell them a draft had been coming through. I just couldn't bear looking at that open hole, like an open wound in the body of our home.

I turned up the radio and tried to dance, concentrating on the bass guitar and the way it rumbled down low in my stomach.

What would I tell Brian when we did talk? My father, the one who can't stand you, punches holes in walls when he gets steamed?

I could hear Brian's reaction now. "Josie," he'd say, "that's demented."

His dad, the cop, says more murders occur between husbands and wives than any other group in society. He hates being called in to break up domestic disputes, because — he says — they're more unpredictable than bank robberies. One of his partners was killed when he tried to stop a sailor from beating his wife to death with a crowbar.

I thought, if Brian finds out — maybe he'll dump me. But then again, I couldn't keep secrets from him the way Marsha and Dad were keeping them from me. I'd have to tell him sometime. I *needed* to tell him before I exploded!

Switching off the radio, I decided what I had to do, which was get to the bottom of this craziness. If people wouldn't level with me, I'd find out what was going on for myself.

I started by pulling everything out of the kitchen cupboards. I knew exactly what I was looking for: liquor (Vodka, probably. No stink.) or packets of white powder or joints or pills. All I found was an open bottle of white wine that Marsha uses for cooking when she's in her gourmet mood. In the unfinished side of the basement there were boxes and boxes of Chrissy's old clothes and some of mine, too, that hadn't worn through. They were just outgrown. Marsha always claims she's saving them for the Salvation Army. But they've been there at least two years.

I tipped over the first box — ran upstairs when I thought I'd heard a car pull up, then down again when it turned out to be a neighbor's — dumped another. Frantically I searched through every pants pocket, pulled socks inside out, shook shirts and shoes. I searched the den, too, which was also in the basement. If Dad had stashed stuff on that floor, I would have found it.

In the bathroom cabinet upstairs were some expired prescriptions that should have been thrown out. They looked as if they hadn't been touched in years. That was all though. And Chrissy's room was clean. Which left my parents' room.

I ransacked both closets. Next came the six drawers under the bed, and the two bureaus. My father's was a tall one; the only drawer without clothes in it was the one on the bottom. He'd reserved that for old papers, insurance forms, and medical records. If he was sick and had been to a doctor I might find something here, I thought.

I took my time, although every two minutes I jumped up and ran to look out Chrissy's window. If Marsha found me snooping in Dad's papers, she'd strangle me. If Dad found me . . . I just didn't know what he'd do anymore. And I didn't want to.

Under all that were his military records, from the time when he'd been in the army while I was a baby. There was a photo of him in his uniform. He looked very young and had sort of a silly expression on his face, as if he was being told to be serious and didn't really want to. I thought he looked really handsome.

I couldn't remember him in uniform. According to his release papers, I was about ten months old when he left the army. He'd been a first lieutenant then. And there were two little brown-colored stars knocking around in the bottom of the drawer. I shut it, feeling exasperated. There didn't seem to be anything among his things or anyone else's that explained his behavior. If he'd hidden anything in the house, it sure wasn't there now.

Later in the afternoon Marsha called to say that she and Chrissy were on their way home so that I could have the car to get to work. I managed to finish both algebra assignments but didn't have time for anything else before changing into my Harvey's uniform. When I put the completed work in my homework folder, the French test was there, where I'd left it. I took one look at the red ink D on the first page. Wondering if Mary really believed I'd done well on it, I crumpled it into a tight wad, then tossed it into the wastebasket beside my bed.

I didn't even promise myself I'd do better on the next one. I no longer felt able to judge how my brain was going to work when I asked it to.

At Harvey's the crowd was light. We all took long breaks to make the night go faster. At closing, Sanville passed out the paychecks. I always deposited half in my savings account for college; the rest was spending money, but that included school lunches and most of my clothes.

There was a twenty-four-hour Instabank at the end of the shopping center. But I'd wait until the next day when it was light. A couple of people had been mugged there last winter after dark.

I decided to call Brian from a pay phone on the way home though. I wouldn't be able to explain any of this over the phone, but at least I could tell him how much I needed to see him, alone.

# CHAPTER EIGHT

FRIDAY NIGHT WE SAT ON THE BREAKWATER. I STUFFED my hands into my Levi's pockets and gasped at each cold blast off the ocean. The fog over the waves was thick. It felt as if ice crystals were mixed with the mist. When I blinked, tiny droplets slid off my lashes and rolled down my cheeks.

" 'The white waves paced to and fro in the moonlight,' " I whispered, " 'and the wind brought the sound of the great sea's voice.' "

Brian reached over and smoothed the blond tangles away from my eyes. He looked into them searchingly. "Which one is that?" he asked.

"Stephen Crane," I said, pretending I didn't know that both of us were nervous. It had been my idea to come here instead of going to Michelle's party. But, as much as I'd wanted to talk to Brian the other night, actually doing it seemed incredibly difficult. I still hadn't told him I wouldn't be able to see him anymore. I didn't know how I was going to do it — or if I would at all. The main thing was, I didn't want to hurt him. The wind whipped hair into my mouth. I drew it out with one finger.

"You like to quote writers and poets," he observed.

"I like thinking that whatever I've seen or am doing right now, someone else has been there before me or had thoughts about it."

"Not very adventuresome," he commented. "Don't you ever want to be the first to do something really special?"

"Like walk on Venus? Or throw a Frisbee off Mount Everest?"

He laughed, the sound of his clear voice coming straight back on the wind. Without meaning to, I wondered what it would be like to never hear it again. Thinking about us like that made me incredibly sad.

"I just like to know what's coming up," I said over a lump in my throat. "I like to know where I stand." If I started crying in front of him, now, I'd blow everything.

We sat on the rocks and the wind died down some, but not enough. I'd worn a bulky sweater, but the knit let sharp slivers of wind slip through. Brian took off his jacket and laid it over my shoulders.

"Now you'll be cold," I told him.

He shrugged.

We talked about school some, and his brothers and sister, who is in kindergarten. When his lips turned blue, we climbed back to the beach and crossed the parking lot to the Zbierski House. The town had bought it several years ago and converted it into a daytime senior center. Police cruisers make rounds of the parking lot and flash their headlights across the building each time around — just to be sure no one has broken in or is sleeping on town property. There's a wide railed porch on three sides. The side away from the water is always a good ten degrees warmer. We sat out of sight, on the porch floor, our backs to the peeling gray clapboards.

"Can't see the submarines from here." Brian faked a grumble.

I laughed. "No. But at least I have you all to myself."

"It was just you, me, and the sea gulls a few minutes ago."

"Too much competition," I whispered, and felt like being as close to him as I could. I swiveled on the seat of my jeans and nestled my head in his lap. He looked down on me and his eyes were so soft and so dark that almost all of the blue seemed gone.

"What did my father say to you?" I asked.

"Just that you couldn't talk to me. Then he hung up."

I nodded. It could have been worse.

"Did you tell him to say that, Josie?" he asked quietly. "Did you ask him to get rid of me?"

"Of course not, dummy."

"But you didn't want to talk to me before that," he said. "And you didn't call me back." Then I knew he was hurting.

"It's not that I didn't want to. I just couldn't." I shifted onto one hip so I was no longer looking up into his confused eyes.

"You said you wanted to meet me down here on the beach, that you couldn't go to the party tonight," he went on. "Or, maybe it's more like you didn't *want* to go. With me anyway."

"Brian, I . . ." He turned me back again to face him, holding my chin still, so he could see my eyes.

"The truth," he said, so softly the wind carried away all but the shape of the words on his lips. One finger touched my cheek in silent warning. I wanted him to kiss me, but I knew he was too upset. Tears stung the backs of my lids.

He drew his finger away and there was an angry edge to his voice this time. "You know we've always been honest, Josie. Tell me. They've finally gotten to you, haven't they?"

"Who? What?"

"Who, what," he grunted and shoved my head off his lap. He went to stand hunched over the white rail, his arms resting along it. I thought he looked a lot like an old sailor, deliberating on the tides. "Your friends. You just don't want to be seen with me."

"Brian Pedersen!" I shouted to make sure he was listening, then stood up in a hurry. "You've always been the one hung up on what other people think of us. I really don't give a damn!"

"Then, why are we here, on the beach in November, freezing our buns off instead of curled up warm and cozy on your friend's couch?"

A piece of truth was all I could give him for the moment — because that was all I had myself. "My father's taken an irrational dislike to you," I said, watching his expression. "For some reason, he's all of a sudden obsessed with us shooting at River-edge. And he's gotten it into his head that you're some kind of dangerous influence on me. He doesn't want me to see you . . . for a while," I finished softly.

"How long," Brian asked slowly, "is *a while?*"

I looked down at the gray-painted planks, spotted with sea gull droppings. "Just until I can convince him otherwise."

"In other words, he's ordered you to break up with me."

I just stared at him, and what seemed like a long time passed while he thought about that. Then he turned and started walking away.

I thought he was heading toward one of the wooden-slatted chairs. But he kept going, down the steps and onto the lawn where green picnic tables are chained to cement blocks sunk in the turf. As if someone is likely to pick up a hundred-pound solid pine table and walk off with it. Brilliant.

"Where are you going?" I shouted.

He turned, his fists bulging in his pockets, and stared furiously at me in the moonlight. "That's an excuse," he shouted into the wind.

"No, it's not!"

He thought for a minute, then took one step toward the porch.

"Listen," he began, "I'll have a talk with your old man and square everything away. Then I'll take you somewhere special — to your homecoming dance maybe, with dinner at the Lighthouse Inn before."

"No," I said quickly. "That wouldn't work." I could just picture Brian standing in front of my father, trying to reason with him. And I could see that big, clenched fist heading straight for Brian's face — and impacting as violently as it had on the sheet of wallboard. I couldn't let Brian near him.

"You don't want me to take you out, then. Right, Josie?"

"I — I didn't say that. I said no for now because I need time. Please, Bri — "

"Forget it!" he yelled, backing away rapidly. "Just forget all about us!"

I tore after him, down the wooden steps and across the coarse gray dead grass.

"Okay!" I gasped, holding on to his arm. "Okay. It's like this. I don't know why he's dumping on you out of the blue, Brian. I honestly don't. I love you. I'd never say anything to make you look bad. But he's just got . . . I don't know, got this one sick idea in his head about you and guns, and about something . . . about *you* hurting me and Chrissy."

"That doesn't make sense."

"Of course it doesn't. But he's been acting awfully strange lately. I don't know what he'll pull next." There was no way to get around it now. I told him about the 7-Eleven, and about how Dad almost hit me.

Brian calmed down awfully fast after that. "He must be on something, or else he's sick. You know, emotionally disturbed. He'd have to be to warp out like that." Brian looked very worried, but not in a critical way. "He's never done anything like this before, has he?"

"Of course not," I said, and hugged him hard. He was saying exactly what I'd been thinking, but it made me feel better just to hear somebody else say it out loud. Like when it's really dark in a strange place, and whoever you're with says it's spooky, then you know what you're feeling is normal and you're not being a baby.

"He doesn't drink a lot, does he?" Brian asked.

"Hardly at all." Although Brian's body was blocking the worst of the wind, I shivered.

Brian noticed. "You still cold? I should have brought a blanket in the car." He sounded angry with himself, which was funny when you thought about it.

"To a party. Bring a blanket. Now that would have looked logical."

He smiled. "Pajama party?"

I shook my head and grimaced. "Anyway, I don't know what would make my father behave like this."

"Drugs," he suggested without changing his expression.

"I ransacked the entire house. Nothing."

"Did you look in his car? A lot of addicts stash their supply somewhere other than their house."

"No," I said. "But I will."

He took me home at midnight, which we figured was a reasonable hour for Michelle's party to break up. But we parked on Mary's side of the block and I cut through the backyards. If anyone was waiting for me, it would look as if I'd come home with her. No one was up.

I made myself instant coffee, boiling the water in a mug in the microwave. Sitting in the kitchen, I sipped slowly; the shivering kept up a long time after I stopped being cold. I sat over the steaming mug, grateful that Brian was trying to understand and hadn't been turned off by Dad's problems. I thought about my father for a long time.

At last I remembered why Stephen Crane had popped into my head. When we'd studied *The Red Badge of Courage* a couple of years ago, Dad had told me it was his favorite book. He'd said he read it three or four times all the way through while he was in the hospital. I hadn't questioned him then, but, now that I thought about it, I couldn't recall him ever being in a hospital.

Maybe he'd had his tonsils out when he was a kid. I mean, it might have been before I was around. Or maybe it had been when I was too little to remember, or when he was away in the army. After all, that wasn't the sort of thing a person looked back on and brought up in ordinary conversation.

But, whenever it had happened, I suspected it was still another part of a secret I wasn't meant to know. And I resented Marsha all the more because she was trying to pretend nothing was wrong. I wasn't going to let her keep doing that, I decided.

# CHAPTER NINE

SOMETIMES YOU KNOW HOW THE DAY WILL GO JUST BY the morning sounds. Crickets chirruping, lawn mowers grating, soft rain running down the bedroom window — these are all good omens. Marsha's dippy exercise music is good, because it's normal. The scratchy sound of her scrubbing out pans is not. She hates cleaning them and stockpiles roasting pans and saucepans in the drawer under the oven for when she's in a monster mood.

I followed the noise to the kitchen and poured myself a glass of orange juice from one of the plastic containers in the fridge, took a sip, then wrinkled my nose.

"This tastes lousy," I said, not blaming her or anything. Just stating the truth. "Is it spoiled or something?"

"I've changed brands," she replied, without turning away from the sink. "The frozen kind is less expensive."

"Since when are you so worried about money?"

She ignored my question. "This kind has just as much vitamin C as the fancy ones."

"Oh," I said.

She wore an aqua jogging suit. With her orange red hair, I thought, she looked like a logo for Howard Johnson's. I was grinning into the glass at my private joke when she spun around suddenly.

"Where were you last night, Josephine?"

The pulp clung to the insides of the glass and I studied each speck thoroughly, as if this was a good gauge of orange juice quality.

"I told you I was invited to Michelle's party." Well, I had been. So that wasn't actually a lie.

"Yes." Her voice was taut and low. "You said you'd be walking to Mary's house last night and from there you were going to the Vonnegut girl's party. But Mary called at nine-thirty. She was worried when you didn't show."

Oops, I said silently, thinking how dumb I'd been not to cover for myself ahead of time. I just wasn't used to deceiving people.

Marsha was giving me her look-me-in-the-eye-and-deny-this-one glare. "You were with Brian," she stated, "after your father told you not to see him."

I would have poured the last inch of juice, which was mostly pulp anyway, down the drain and stomped out of the kitchen. But that reminded me of Dad's parting scene the other day. And I hadn't liked that.

"You don't honestly agree with him. Do you?" I asked. "*You* don't think I should stop seeing Brian."

"Yes," she answered straight away. "I do."

"Bull!" I stood up and clapped the glass down hard on the suds-slick Formica. "That's just part of a parental united front. You know Brian Pedersen; how could be possibly do me any harm?"

"He could and he already has," she said firmly.

I stared at her. "What?"

"I saw your French test, Josie. I'm not happy about that grade and wonder how many others you've slipped by us."

Her voice was shaking, as if she might start crying any minute. My god! I thought. It's just one lousy French test. Then it hit me —

"You went in my room! You were snooping through

67

my trash can!" I accused her, feeling the heat rise inch by inch over my throat and face.

She shook her head. "Chrissy dragged your waste-basket into the hall and dumped it on the floor. But *that*," she said, extending a warning finger, "is beside the point. We have a rule that all tests are seen before they're tossed."

"I can't believe this!" I wailed. "Your husband is busting up walls and falling down helpless in the road — and you're getting on my case for a test grade?" From the look on her face, I knew I'd gone too far.

"Look, Josephine Ann Monroe," she shouted, suddenly beyond anger and into fury. "I can't handle teen rebellions on top of everything else, your father's behavior included!"

Almost immediately, though, Marsha seemed to shrink; her shoulders appeared suddenly too small for the aqua sweat suit. She rarely yelled at anyone. She rarely let herself get worked up to the point of exploding. Marsha let things work themselves out. Two weeks ago, she'd have looked at that grade and sympathized; we'd have laughed it off together as a fluke. Imagine, Josie Monroe pulling a D. But now Marsha looked like a deflated balloon.

"There are things you don't understand," she said shakily, threw the SOS pad into the sink, and stalked past me into the living room where she sat heavily on the couch.

I followed and, pulling an embroidered throw pillow into my stomach, hugged it, then sat on the floor.

"Might help if somebody told me what is going on," I said, making my voice quieter for her.

She thought about that for a minute or two, then

sighed. "I may get myself a job. They're looking for part-time cashiers at the grocery store where I shop."

I squinted at her. This didn't seem to have much to do with Dad pummeling plaster or hating Brian. On the other hand, it was not exactly the kind of news Dad would greet with enthusiasm. He and Marsha sort of have a pact about her being at home at least until Chrissy is in first grade. Even after then, I suspected he'd be sensitive about her starting up a career. After what had happened with my mother.

I looked out the front window. Dad's car was gone. "Does Dad know?"

"I think . . . he realizes it must happen," she answered noncommittally.

"Why do you have to get a job? Are you tired of being home with Chrissy?" That, I could understand. Chasing after the little turkey could get to anyone. If Dad was insisting that she stay home, and she didn't really want to — that wasn't fair.

She smiled dimly and shook her red curls. "No. I like being home. I never intended to pursue a full-time career. That's just not me."

*You* is picking fresh strawberries, making jam, taking Chrissy to story hour, I mused silently. And jogging down to the beach every day. I liked her more than I wanted to say, or even think about.

"So, why work?" I asked. "Money? Is Dad losing his job or something?" That could account for a lot of his tension.

She looked at me straight on. Her green eyes were shadowed and serious. "I hope not. But, you see, he's missed a lot of time at the office. So his commissions aren't very dependable. That's hard to budget around."

"But you said he hasn't been sick," I reminded her.

69

And I *knew* he hadn't been at home, unless he'd sneaked back in the middle of the day while I was in school. That didn't make sense either. So if he wasn't at work or at home — where was he?

Marsha shrugged, dropping her glance. "It's more as if he needs time to himself, Josie, to work things out."

"What things?"

"Oh," she said. "The past. He was in Vietnam, you know that. He's never talked much about his army days to me. But I think it was very hard on him. More than he lets on."

Come to think of it, he'd told me almost nothing about those years, even though he loved to go on and on, telling me stuff about when he was a kid growing up in Vermont on a dairy farm.

Marsha lifted her green eyes from the carpet and fixed them on me. "Stay away from Brian for a while, Josie . . . for me. I know it doesn't make much sense, but if your father can stop brooding about the boy, maybe he'll be able to concentrate better on his work. The best we can do for him now is to give him some space."

*Rebellion.* I thought later about Marsha's words. Am I rebelling by caring for Brian, and wanting to be with him? *I* didn't think so. And I didn't think there was really anything logically or illogically wrong with Brian from my father's point of view. He was reacting to something else, and I had to find out what that was.

MARSHA DID HER ERRANDS IN THE MORNING, THEN LEFT the car for me and walked Chrissy over to a neighbor's. Since it was Saturday, I had to be at Harvey's at noon.

I left home early and, on the way, stopped at Hartford National.

The line snaked between velvet-covered ropes that made the place look like a theater lobby instead of a bank. I got at the end, and while I waited, started filling in the deposit slip. Half to savings for college, half to cash. Like always.

There were only three tellers, and they moved as if their batteries had run down. The line inched forward and I looked around at the faces of strangers; every one of them glared impatiently at a teller.

When I reached the head of the line, I endorsed the back of the check and slowly slid it across the high partition, toward a young woman wearing a soft navy sweater and a string of pearls. But I held on to the deposit slip.

"May I help you?" she asked, a shade of irritation in her voice. As if I was the one who was holding up every person there.

I felt the triplicate sheets of the deposit slip in my left hand, then quickly crumpled them.

"Cash," I told her. "All cash, please."

# CHAPTER TEN

TUESDAY AFTER SCHOOL I FOUND A NOTE MARSHA HAD left under a refrigerator magnet shaped like a cauliflower. It said that she'd be out shopping with Chrissy for the afternoon. Dad wasn't around either. I'd seen very little of him since the night he'd blown up at me, and we hadn't spoken to each other at all.

I decided it was lucky they'd all taken off. I definitely

didn't want to be alone with Dad. His unpredictable moods scared me. And I still didn't totally trust Marsha. This suspicious voice at the back of my brain kept nagging at me, making me wonder if Marsha had only told me what she wanted me to know, leaving out the worst.

Besides, there were some things I wanted to do, and while they were gone was the perfect time to do them.

I phoned Mary. "Are you busy for the next couple of hours?" I asked.

"Not really." She sounded surprised I'd called her.

"Come over, then. I need help." And I hung up before she could ask any questions.

While I waited for her, I searched out a snack for both of us. This time I didn't bother checking the fridge but went straight to the cupboards. Bad news there, too. We were even out of Lipton Onion Soup Mix — which Marsha always keeps around for making dip or pouring over a pot roast. I grabbed a dozen saltines and made sandwiches with peanut butter, then walked down to the basement and out the back way into the cold November air.

Mary met me as I was locking the door. "What's up?"

I handed her three of the sandwiches. "We're going shopping."

"No car?"

"They're both in use. And I have to do this now."

"If you say so." She took a bite of cracker sandwich and shot me a sideways look as we walked. "I'm sorry, Josie. I feel so stupid."

I knew, of course, what she meant. "I should have told you I wouldn't be going to Michelle's party. It was my fault."

"Did you get in trouble?"

"Not really," I fibbed. She'd only feel worse.

"Well, I'm glad. If something I did broke you and Brian up, I'd never forgive myself."

"I know," I said.

The street around the corner from Tyler is a dead end. Past the barrier marked with reflective strips are woods, then a field that's partially submerged in salt water when the tide comes in. At low tide, though, it's flat land with tall grasses and sandy banks. The place smells of concentrated brine. Redwinged blackbirds and a couple of clumsy-looking gray cranes nest among the reeds.

If you know where to step, you can cross the swamp on foot. On the other side is a shopping center with a Stop & Shop, liquor store, Radio Shack, and dry cleaner. We'd caught it at low tide luckily. While we walked, I told her about my father's latest flare up over Brian — and how he'd almost slugged me.

With the money from my paycheck, we bought enough food to fill two sacks. That was all we could carry back across the swamp, and anyway that left me with only five dollars. Mary helped me put everything away — orange juice (the decent kind in a carton), fresh hamburger, a whole chicken, eggs, luncheon meat, cheese, bread, and Chrissy's staple, Spaghetti-Os.

We sat at the kitchen table and had a cup of tea to warm up.

"The house is a wreck," I said. "That's the other thing I want to do, clean up before they get home."

"I'll help," Mary offered without being asked.

"You don't have to. I just felt like having company."

I smiled, but didn't tell her she was there for a better reason.

"I want to. What with Marty and all . . . well, you and I haven't seen too much of each other." She smiled, and I thought, She really is a good friend, as funny as she is sometimes.

Lots of newspapers were piled up on the glass coffee table. Chrissy's toys lay around every room in colorful splotches. The carpet was tracked over with dead leaves and stuff. Dad would have a fit if he saw the place. I guessed Marsha had already started working some-where and was too tired to keep up with the cleaning. She obviously hadn't said anything about the job to Dad. Wise move, I thought, under the circumstances.

I tied a kerchief over my hair to keep the dust out of it, gathered up newspapers for the trash, put away Chrissy's toys, and dusted while Mary vacuumed. We finished the downstairs pretty fast and started on the bedrooms. Marsha and Dad's was last.

"I'll put away the vacuum," Mary offered. "It goes in the basement. Right?"

"Thanks. Then come back up here."

When she walked back into the bedroom, I was sit-ting on the floor in front of Dad's bureau with the bottom drawer open and half its contents spread out on the carpet around me.

"What are you doing?" she asked, frowning.

"These are some of my father's papers, from back when he was in the army."

Her voice lowered to a whisper. "Are you supposed to be looking at his stuff?" she asked, her eyes huge.

"No."

"Well, hadn't you better put it back before they get home?"

"After I have a good look. After I find what I need. That's why you're here."

She shook her head five or six times and backed toward the hallway. "No, Josie. I don't like this. You said your Dad has been hyper lately. And he almost hit you the other night, for hardly any reason at all. What do you think he'd do if he found us snooping?"

"Go watch for his car," I told her firmly.

She groaned. "Do I have to?"

"Definitely," I mumbled, shuffling through photos and forms.

I found a newspaper clipping among the top layer of stuff that I'd set aside. I scanned the article; some of the sentences had been underlined in ink.

"Anyone in sight yet?" I shouted.

"No-o-o-o." Mary's weak moan drifted up from the living room. "Oh, Josie, hurry up. I don't like this."

"I'm done. I just have to put all this away," I said reassuringly, stuffing papers back, trying to remember the order they'd been in so it wouldn't look as if somebody had been pawing through them.

By the time I got down to the living room, Mary's face was white. She gnawed on her lower lip. "I gotta go now." She headed for the back door.

I grabbed her by the arm. "Please stay. Just till we read through this together. It's what I've been looking for."

"Oh, Josie, I don't know." She glanced past me, longingly, at the door. But in spite of her nervousness, her eyes dropped curiously to the ratty piece of newspaper in my hand. "Why is that so important?"

"It proves that what Marsha told me is right . . . and that those jerks at the Seven-Eleven are wrong. Look here," I said, and sat down in the middle of the living room carpet. "See how the article is worn along the fold lines? Just as if it's been carried around for a long time in a wallet."

Mary's eyes met mine. "Your dad?"

"I don't see who else. Marsha hardly ever reads the newspaper. And if she'd been carrying it around with her, she wouldn't put it in Dad's drawer when she was done with it. That's his private place; she keeps all her things in a shoebox in her closet."

"Let me see," said Mary. She took the article gently and read in silence while I peeked over her shoulder at the words. "This is so sad," she said after a long time.

The article was about some veterans who were visiting the Vietnam War Memorial in Washington, D.C., to honor their friends who'd died in the war. One man said he still remembered the name of every man in his platoon. Another said he'd been wounded and taken by helicopter to a hospital, then sent home. So he never found out if his friends had made it through the war. Twenty years later, he was reading the names of the dead on the wall, hoping he wouldn't find any he recognized.

"So many men died over there," I murmured.

"And they weren't all Americans," said Mary, her dark eyes moist.

I swallowed and nodded. The article didn't mention any Vietnamese casualties. I felt sick and embarrassed. Mary's ancestors had come from that part of the world. Squeezing her hand, I let her know I was sorry.

"Look at this part at the end," I said, pointing. "It's all underlined. It says that veterans' organizations still believe men who were in the army and marines in Vietnam are more likely to develop medical problems because they were exposed to Agent Orange, a chemical sprayed on the jungle to kill trees and make it easier to find snipers."

"You think he's sick or something?" Mary asked.

"I don't know," I said, after giving that some thought. "But the fact that my father's been carrying around this article at least shows he's been brooding about the war. And, right here, it also talks about men having higher rates of stress and psychological symptoms, some of them serious, that relate to their being in the war."

Mary looked worried. "I wonder just how *serious* they mean."

I patted her on the shoulder. "You know" — I got up, feeling better than I had in days — "this is good news, in a way."

"Good that your father might be seriously ill?"

"No, silly. Good that he's not an addict or turning mean for no reason. Maybe he's been feeling bad lately. He reads about this Agent Orange stuff and gets scared. Maybe he even worries that he's passed something on to me and Chrissy. I mean, he might feel so guilty about it that he'd just go bonkers." My imagination was working quickly. "And he'd probably swear Marsha to silence."

"I suppose so," said Mary doubtfully. "Don't you think you'd better put that article away now?"

To make her feel better, I did. But I couldn't help digging down between the papers to finger the star-shaped medals at the bottom. They meant he'd done something good and brave. He'd been a hero, only he didn't like to talk about it. Feeling proud, I covered the stars tenderly with his discharge papers. My father's last day in the army had been July 18, 1971.

I ran down the stairs in twos. "I can't wait to tell

Brian!" I squealed. Kicking off my shoes, I switched on the radio. An old Petula Clark tune blasted through the house.

Mary laughed. "You'd better turn that down."

"Why?" I began dancing circles around her where she sat on the floor. I spun, scrunching my toes in the carpeting, grinning at the ceiling as it rotated overhead. "Those jerks are wrong, now there won't be any hassle," I belted aloud my own lyrics, drowning out Petula.

Everything was going to be better now. I had a handle on this thing that was wedging itself between us. If Dad was sick, I'd make him go to a doctor. If he needed to see a psychiatrist or counselor of some kind, I'd find one for him. At least I was beginning to understand why he might act the way he had. It must have something to do with Vietnam.

After a while Mary joined in singing. We sounded horrible, screeching nastily, laughing, making up new lines.

Neither of us heard the car pull into the driveway. But the slam of the Seville's door made us both stop and stare at each other.

I glanced out the bay window. Dad was on his way up the walk; I flicked off the radio.

"I really should go now," Mary murmured.

"No," I said quickly. "He'll see you slipping out and think we've been doing something wrong. Just stay long enough to say hello, then you can sort of casually mention your mom needs you home to set the dinner table or something."

"Okay," she said nervously.

"Don't worry. He won't do anything weird while you're here."

Regardless of what I told her, she still hung a couple steps behind me. At the last minute, I couldn't stand still, just waiting for him. I ran to the front door and flung it open. Because I knew the truth, because I knew a part of what was going on in his head, we could talk now!

"Hi!" I said brightly as he stepped inside.

He froze in the doorway, peering down at me. And that sickening cloudiness slowly spread over the surface of his eyes. I shivered and felt my palms grow moist. I didn't turn around to see what Mary was doing.

He was mumbling something that sounded like baby talk gibberish: *"Gai que, gai que . . ."* Then he slowly reached out toward the kerchief on my head.

"Josie," whimpered Mary in warning.

I stepped back out of his reach, feeling ashamed for being afraid of my own father. "It's all right," I murmured, for Mary, for him, and for me.

*"Gai que.* No. Oh, no!" Dad sounded as if he was choking. His eyes were enormous, horrified, suddenly trained on Mary. He withdrew his outstretched hand and raked it in agitation through his hair, then suddenly bolted for the stairs. A moment later we heard his door slam.

In silence Mary stared at me, and I stared back. I was choking and had to sit down. Mary cleared her throat.

"Look, Josie," she said softly, hastily, "I don't want to hurt your feelings. But that man is . . . crazy. If I were you, I'd get out of this house and call the police. This minute."

"No." I pressed my hands to my eyes, trapping the tears. No way was I going to start bawling now. I had to handle this. "No, he just needs some help. Marsha and I will find out who can help him. Maybe a doctor."

When I opened my eyes, Mary was halfway out the kitchen door.

"Where are you going?"

"Josie," she hissed, her eyes darting desperately toward the steps, "you saw how he looked at me. He was pretty spacey when he walked in and saw *you*. But one glance at *me*, and he whacked out completely. You know why that is, don't you?"

A sinking feeling, like being in an elevator going down at supersonic speed, hit me in the stomach. "You remind him of the people in Vietnam . . ."

She nodded emphatically. "I'm scared, Josie. Don't ask me to come over anymore. I can't."

"But, Mary, what if — "

"Just *don't*!" she insisted. "If you want to talk, call on the phone or come over to my house. But don't ask me to come here."

And before I could say anything more she'd slipped away.

I collapsed in a lump on the sofa. What was I going to do? Call the police? I couldn't do that to my own father. Besides, things weren't that bad. Were they? Mary tended to blow things out of proportion; she got hysterical easily. Maybe it was true that she reminded Dad of the Asian women he'd seen. But once he calmed down, I was sure we could talk.

I waited an hour, trying to decide if I should go upstairs. Marsha still wasn't home. I was worried Dad would ask me if I knew where she was. Should I make something up if he did?

I pulled off the kerchief and got dressed for Harvey's, then checked the time. If Marsha didn't get home soon, I'd be late — unless I took Dad's car. But I wasn't allowed to do that. He might get a call from a client, and he wouldn't want to drive them around in Marsha's heap. Of course, he didn't seem in good enough shape to drive anyone anywhere, so . . .

I looked up from the kitchen table where I was having coffee. Dad stood in the doorway.

"Hi," he said.

I held my breath. "Hi." It came out and drifted away, leaving silence between us.

"Any more of that?" he asked, sounding almost bashful.

"In the coffee brewer," I told him and sipped from my cup. Did I dare ask him about his reaction to Mary? No, I thought. Not yet.

He poured himself a cup and sat down across the table from me. After a few minutes he pushed the cup away and watched my face.

"Were you here when I got home?" he asked in a quiet voice.

"Oh, Dad," I groaned.

"I take that as a yes?" He gave a little chuckle, as if he was making fun of himself. As if it had just slipped his mind, or he'd been too busy to notice.

"We have to talk," I told him, trying to keep my voice steady. "It was like you weren't even there, inside your own body. You walked in, and Mary was with me, and you didn't recognize me."

He swore under his breath and looked away from my eyes. "Josie, listen. I'm sorry. It won't happen again. I'm really whipped from work and — "

"That's not it," I interrupted.

He was silent for a while. Then he sighed. "I've got a lot on my mind, I guess. You shouldn't have to deal with this. You're just a kid and . . ."

"What's *gai que?*" I demanded.

The word seemed to stop him short. Confusion, then fear flashed across his eyes. "Did I call Mary that?"

"Me, I think. You didn't seem to notice her at first. You were muttering strange words and called me *gai que*. What is it?" I persisted. I wasn't going to be satisfied with making no headway at all. Even finding out a little bit would be better than nothing.

He stared at me, frowning as if this was an unexpected and especially troubling piece of news to him. But his eyes remained clear and in focus.

"A *gai que*," he said, "is a young woman who lives in a village."

"In the Vietnamese language," I said, to make sure I understood.

"Yes."

"But . . . well, I have blond hair and light-colored eyes. I can't possibly look like a Vietnamese."

"No," he admitted, sounding as if each word was weighed, "but you are about the age of . . . of . . ." He didn't seem capable of going on.

"The same age as some of the soldiers you had to fight?" I asked. In history we'd studied the Vietnam War. The book had said that many of the Communist soldiers were just teenagers.

"Yes," he said quickly. "That must be it."

"But," I began, "you left the army a long time ago. Why should it start bothering you now when — "

There was a clatter at the front door and Marsha burst through, gasping for breath. "Oh, Josie," she cried, tugging Chrissy along behind her. "I'm so sorry, we got held up by traffic. Now here's the key, and you'd better hurry. I may have made you late for work as it is."

I looked at Dad.

"I'm fine," he said, smiling as if his cheeks would split. "Better get going."

A part of me wanted the excuse to be out of the house. Another part wanted to stay and keep talking. There was more, I was sure. But I knew he had shut me out for the time being. So perhaps there was no reason to feel I should stay.

# CHAPTER ELEVEN

WHEN I GOT TO HARVEY'S, MARY WAS ALREADY THERE. "I didn't know you were working tonight. How come you didn't call?" I asked. "I'd have given you a ride."

She dropped her eyes and pulled loose the end of her apron string, then retied it, watching the bow over her shoulder. "Marty drove me."

"Oh," I murmured.

"I would have offered you a lift," she said quickly, "but we had to stop at the dry cleaner and drugstore for Marty's mom on the way. We figured you wouldn't want to be bothered with that. You know, being dragged around town."

"Sure," I said.

"You aren't mad at me, Josie? Are you?" she asked, her black eyes bright, but then she hurried on as if she didn't really want an answer. "I mean, I didn't think Marty and I should just pull up out front, with your dad being . . . well, so edgy. And if he answered the phone I wouldn't know what to say."

"You could ask for me," I grumbled. "It's not as if he's going to do anything to hurt you, for crying out loud." I stacked clean coffee cups in the little elevator rack that pushed them up through a hole in the counter.

Mary moved over beside me. "I don't know how you can be sure about that, Josie. You read what that newspaper said: Serious psychological symptoms. I mean, he seemed pretty intense to me. I don't think he knew where he was at all."

"Don't worry about it."

She shook her head. "I can't help worrying. You live with him." I didn't say anything. "Look," she went on, "Marty's coming back around nine. He'll stay till closing. You want a ride home?" she asked, but I sensed she didn't really want me to accept.

"No, I have Marsha's car," I told her.

I envied Mary. There wasn't much chance of Brian stopping by. He was probably still upset with me, I thought dismally. I picked up my pad and pencil and started to turn away.

Mary grabbed me by the arm. "You aren't mad at me, Josie? About not wanting to come over because of your dad."

"Of course not," I told her.

"I mean . . ." I saw in her eyes that she was trying to make me understand something beyond her words. "I was scared, Josie. I don't know how you stay in the house with someone like that. Aren't you terrified?"

"He's my father," I said simply.

But she was right. A part of me was frightened. However, another knew him from when there were only the two of us and I'd ride around with him while he took clients to see houses. I'd sit next to him in the front seat, with the strangers in the back, and listen to him tell them all about the "perky Cape Cod" they'd be seeing next — the two-and-a-half baths, the field-stone fireplace, Kitchen-Aid dishwasher, and upgrade carpet. And sometimes he'd wink secretively at me so that I'd know *he knew* he was exaggerating to make the place sound glamorous.

Back then he'd been my closest friend. Whether there were just the two of us or, later, with Marsha and Chrissy as well, he'd been the glue that held us Monroes together. But now everything was changing; he'd almost become the enemy.

I thought, how much easier it is to fight someone when you don't love them. Then you don't have so many mixed-up feelings about what you have to do.

Later, Marty did show up. He had three other guys from the team with him, and they lounged in a booth and ordered platters with extra sides of onion rings and ranch fries. Mary nearly tripped over herself getting their meals to them in record time, beaming cheerily all the while.

I felt positively sick. "Probably won't leave a tip," I muttered sarcastically.

"Hmm?" She glanced across the grill, sweeping by with a dizzy expression on her face.

"Nothing." I sighed.

Marty's group was rowdy but seemed sober enough, so Sanville didn't kick them out.

At closing I sat in Marsha's car and waited until I saw Mary come out with Marty hugging her like a big old grizzly bear. As they approached his car, one of Marty's friends got out of the passenger seat and stepped aside. The interior light flashed on, and I saw the other two already sitting in the backseat.

I put my hand on the door latch, but Mary was laughing and slid in next to Marty with the other guy after her, as if she cruised around Groton with four jocks every night of the week.

How she could be scared of my dad but not bat an eye at that crew was beyond me. Well — I enjoyed the morbid thought — if they find her body ditched somewhere in the morning, I'll tell them who did it.

MARSHA AND DAD WERE ARGUING WHEN I GOT HOME. I could hear them before I got out of the car. And inside, it was worse.

"Deceptive!" he was yelling over and over again. "Deceptive bitch! Plotting behind my back!"

Oh, brother, I thought, he's found out about her job.

She was sobbing and ran across the dining room and out through the sliding glass doors onto the deck. He picked up a carved onyx ashtray Uncle Phil had sent us from Naples and heaved it at the wall. Then he took off after her, cussing her out for the whole neighborhood to hear.

"What's with you?" I shouted after them. "Are you both going off the deep end? This place'll look like a hunk of Swiss cheese if you keep it up!"

Then I saw Chrissy.

He was pulling cushions off the couch and setting them up on end around him on the floor, like a fortress.

He looked up solemnly when I peered over the top. "Temple of doom!" he chanted.

"You got that right," I muttered.

I ran across the house to the sliding glass partition and set one foot outside. Marsha whipped around, her face streaked wet, lip quivering, and pointed in the general direction of the second floor. "Inside!" she yelled. "This minute, young lady!"

I backed off, feeling the whole world swell up in my throat. Dad was calling Marsha more names, and she was raving at him, as close to incoherent as I'd ever heard her.

"Come here, Chrissy," I said, holding out my arms above the cushions. I figured if he objected I'd cart the cushions upstairs with us. But he wrapped his plump arms around my neck and buried his nose under my chin while I carried him.

"I'm sorry I yelled at you the other day," I said softly into his ear.

He began to whimper. "Chrissy make a mess — all — all over."

"Sometimes it's fun to make a mess," I told him, hugging his warm chunky body tighter and tighter as we climbed the stairs. "You didn't mean to be bad with the peanut butter."

He was in bed like clockwork every night by eight. It was ten-thirty now, and he wasn't even in pajamas. I didn't want to think what the rest of the night had been like for him.

I changed him into flannel creepers with plastic feet and snapped the elastic around his belly. Then we sat in the antique maple rocker Marsha had used while she was nursing him, and I read to him.

When he fell asleep, I put him in bed and smoothed the covers up to his round chins. I shoved the rocker over closer to his crib, and sat with my eyes shut, trying to ignore *them* — downstairs — still screeching at each other.

"I wish you were older, Chrissy," I whispered, rocking and rocking, focusing on the rhythmic creaks, concentrating on the motion. Maybe I was hoping it would do for me what it had for him — put me to sleep. Make me forget where I was.

I'd never felt like this before. But right at this moment I wished Chrissy was the big brother, and I the little sister. Then all the important decisions would be up to him. And I could depend on him to straighten things out for all of us.

I JUMPED AT THE LOUD BANG, THEN SAT VERY STILL, listening to every little sound in the dark house.

When I'd dropped off to sleep, Marsha and Dad had still been at it. My mouth felt as dry as corkboard, and I gripped the smooth wooden chair arms while I listened. I heard steps retreating quickly down the sidewalk, then softer, lighter ones slowly ascending to the second floor hall.

Good, I thought bitterly. I swallowed over the raw spot in my throat. He's gone. And tears that had stayed put all night welled up and blurred the clown wallpaper in Chrissy's bedroom. "I hope you *never* come back," I whispered. "You bastard."

A few minutes later I pried myself out of the rocker and cautiously tiptoed into the hall. When I peeked into Marsha's room she was standing in front of her bedroom window.

"I'm sorry," I said softly. "He shouldn't be treating you like this. I guess he found out about your job."

She nodded.

"Guess he took it pretty badly."

Marsha smiled dimly. "You could say that." She sighed and turned away from the window. "He's just tired, and worried about his work and you and Chrissy."

"I don't think that's it at all."

She frowned.

"Today, he confused me with a Vietnamese woman.

He totally lost track of who I was, where we were."

Marsha didn't respond.

"We have to *do* something," I insisted. "He's getting worse."

"No!" she answered rigidly. "He's not getting worse. It's just the pressure of everyday life getting to him. It happens all the time to men his age. You just mind your grades and stop giving him a hard time about your boyfriend. He'll calm down. You'll see."

"But — " I began.

"Josie, I'm really tired. We'll talk about this another time. Okay?"

Without answering, I stepped back into the hall and shut her door behind me.

For a while I sat on my bed, then I stretched out flat on my stomach. I couldn't sleep, even though it was nearly twelve. I needed to talk to someone so bad. But Brian would be asleep. If I called I might wake up his mother or father. I couldn't reach Mary by phone either. Her parents had an extension beside their bed, and I knew they'd refuse to let her take a call at this hour.

Everything was so mixed up. And it *was* getting worse, not better. Somebody had to do something.

I guess, in a way, Marsha was just too close to Dad. She loved him and didn't want to blame him for the way he was acting. She wanted to believe that French tests and jobs were the issues. They weren't.


# CHAPTER TWELVE


THE CELLAR DOOR ALWAYS STICKS. MARSHA SAYS IT'S the humidity. But this year the cool, dry November air hadn't made it any better.

After sliding the chain lock out of its track, I carefully pressed one palm flat on the wood next to the knob, braced, and pulled. Unfortunately, as the door groaned open my hand skidded onto the windowpane. There was a soft crack. I swore under my breath. When I lifted my hand, a six-inch triangle of glass came away with it, then smashed on the linoleum.

"Oh, great," I groaned, and waited, listening.

But nobody came down to investigate. I started breathing again.

Stepping carefully around the slivers and out the door, I pulled it closed behind me but made sure it didn't lock. The night was overcast, no moon, very still and dark as the inside of a closet. I remembered the shiny gray slugs that hide deep down among the blades all summer, and wondered if the cold had killed them yet. I'd scream if I stepped on one.

The Chang's house is all on one level, except for the basement. Because both houses are built on a slope, you can walk straight out their cellar door, just like ours. So Mary's bedroom, which is off the back, is a good eight feet above ground.

I pulled out one of the dead forsythia branches Mr. Chang had cut and baled, and reached overhead to scrape it back and forth over Mary's window. Her face appeared, full moon round and white on the other side of the glass. She frowned blindly into the dark until I tapped the branch against the window again. Startled, she jumped back, then at last she saw me and shoved open the window.

"Josie! You scared me half to death. What's wrong?" she demanded, sounding sleepy and grumpy.

I started to open my mouth, then shook my head. Maybe this was a mistake.

"You'd better come inside," she whispered. "Come around to the front. I'll let you in."

I automatically headed through the living room and down the hall toward her room.

"You look awful," she said, trailing two steps behind.

"Thanks a heap." I collapsed on her bed. I shoved a pillow over my face and listened to my pulse thrumming in my ears.

Mary left the room and, a few minutes later, came back carrying a tray loaded with a white-and-blue china teapot and two dainty, handleless cups. She set the tray on an old steamer trunk I'd helped her spray paint magenta and decoupage with faces from old rock posters: Mick Jagger, Rod Stewart, Madonna, Cyndi Lauper. . . .

The rest of the house was decorated with delicate rice paper window shades, silk flower and pussy willow arrangements, squat porcelain vases, and low cushions. White and gold with touches of black lacquer furniture. I often wondered what her refined parents thought of their daughter's taste.

"Do you want sugar?" she asked.

"No."

The cup barely held enough pale brown tea to make three swallows. It wasn't very hot, and I could sip it right away.

We drank tea for what seemed a long time. Mary kept glancing at me from the end of the bed where she sat cross-legged.

"I had to get out of there," I told her at last.

"What happened, Josie?" she asked gently.

I watched the tiny black leaves at the bottom of my cup. "He's crazy. I hate him."

Mary frowned. "Your father?"

I nodded.

"Did he . . . hit you?"

"No. He and Marsha had a terrible fight." And I filled her in on the details.

"I sort of knew there was something going on tonight," she admitted. "We could hear them from our living room." She kept tugging on her bangs, pulling one strand at a time down to her eyebrows. "It must have been awful." She bit her lip and glanced nervously toward her window.

"Nobody saw me leave," I told her.

Mary nodded but didn't look a whole lot reassured.

"I don't want to go back."

"Well, it's about time," she said. "Do you have someplace to go? Relatives nearby?"

I looked at her. She was telling me she didn't want me to stay with her.

"No. Most of them live in California or Michigan. Marsha's sister lives in Philadelphia though." I put the cup down on the tray. "I don't know what to do."

Mary's eyes flickered again toward the window.

"Look," I snapped, "he's not going to kick down your door and grenade your whole family!"

"Okay," she said quickly. "I know. I just . . . what I mean to say is people like that . . . they're somewhat unpredictable."

I groaned and lay back on the bed. "That's the understatement of the year. I don't know, maybe Marsha's right to just let him work out his problem on his own. But if she's wrong, and he only gets worse . . ." How long would Marsha put up with him before she walked out?

I rolled over on my stomach and stuck my face into

the white chenille bedspread. It smelled like Mary's Odyssey perfume. I thought, Josephine Monroe, you made it through losing one mother. You can do it again, if you have to.

But I didn't want to lose Marsha. I suddenly realized how important she'd become to me. And, if she left, Chrissy would go with her.

As if she'd read my mind, Mary asked, "What about Chrissy? Is he upset?"

I lifted my head long enough to rest my chin on one arm. "I don't think he knows anything's wrong. He's just too little."

But he built barricades from couch cushions, so maybe he did. Poor little twerp.

"There must be some sort of treatment center for ex-soldiers who have emotional problems," Mary said quietly. "Maybe in Hartford?"

"Or New York, or else Chicago, or L.A. Suppose that's far enough away?" I demanded, angry because all anyone wanted to do was put distance between themselves and Dad. Then I realized guiltily that that was why I was at Mary's house now.

"Sorry," I mumbled.

"No big deal."

"I'd better go home," I sighed.

"Be careful, Josie," she said when she let me out the front door.

I heard the latch click, then the chain bolt rattle. She was scared, and I wished I had the courage to leave her out of this — for her sake.

I FOUND A BROOM AND DUSTPAN UNDER THE CELLAR stairs and swept up the pieces of broken glass. Then I put the chain back in its slot. I was too numb to be tired, but my stomach felt as empty as if my last meal had been a week ago.

When I got to my room, I looked around at all the familiar things I'd collected over the years. Posters, delicate blown glass figurines of animals and tiny china elves Dad had given me each Christmas from the time I was three, bottles of perfume shaped like flowers, my grandmother's patchwork quilt and the matching embroidered throw pillows Marsha had made for my fourteenth birthday, the photos of Brian and me taken at the boardwalk booth at Ocean Beach Park. Every piece was part of me, of my life, just like Chrissy, Marsha, and Dad were. I wouldn't give up any of them, I decided, tears rolling down my cheeks. I wouldn't . . . wouldn't . . . wouldn't. . . .

# CHAPTER THIRTEEN

AT SCHOOL THE NEXT DAY, SOME JUICY NEW RUMOR WAS circulating. You could see the half-concealed excitement in everyone's eyes and in the way one girl ran up to another in the hall, gasping and talking almost before she'd come to a stop. But, until I got to chemistry, I hadn't given it much thought. And even there, for the first ten minutes, I was distracted by Frankel.

If chemistry weren't a college entrance requirement, everyone would still sign up for it. That's because of Bernard Frankel. Taking his class has all the gruesome fascination of playing Russian roulette.

He shaves his head and wears a lab coat cut to look a lot like a rumpled suit jacket. And when he's asking you a question, he slouches and holds his thumbs and fingers together like a tepee, his beady eyes gleaming at you over his finger-tent. If he sucked on a lollipop he'd be a dead ringer for Kojak in the reruns.

When you don't know an answer, Frankel says, "Now, Mistah Simp-son," looking down his wide nose, making his nostrils flare so you can see the gross spiky hairs inside, "*you* didn't study your notes last night, did you?" Everyone smiles because they know what's coming. "What sort of escapade were you involved in last night, Mis-taaahhh Simpson? What distracted your frenzied, pubescent brain from my lecture? No, no. Let me guess."

And Frankel will invent a totally obscene story about whoever he's talking to and some movie star, or, worse yet, someone else in the class.

It's hysterical for anyone watching. It's even funny for you when it happens to you the first time. But his imagination gets raunchier every time you're the target. You start feeling a little uncomfortable being talked about like that in front of everyone. So you make sure you're ready for Frankel's classes.

That day I sat on my metal stool in front of the black slate bench and lit the gas jet.

Frankel was walking between the benches, his hands balled up behind his back, head down. Pretending to meditate, I thought, but watching, watching us out of the corner of his half-closed eyes, like a barn owl with mice on his mind.

When Frankel reached the other end of the room, Ted Murskey leaned over the narrow trough that split the center of the bench. He whispered in a small, tight voice, "How's it going, Josie?"

I glanced up at him, surprised. He wore wire-rimmed glasses that hung crooked on the bridge of his nose; his eyes always looked distant behind the thick lenses.

Although we'd been in a lot of the same classes since sixth grade, we hardly ever spoke. He'd just always been very shy.

"Fine," I said. "Why?" I slid the tripod over the flame and set a full beaker on it. "Hand me the litmus paper?"

He fumbled for a sheet, trying to find one that wasn't already damp.

"Why did you ask?" I repeated.

"You look tired, sort of."

"I guess I am," I admitted. After getting back from Mary's house, I'd lain awake most of the night. I think I dozed off for a couple of hours near morning. My head was hurting now and my eyes burned. I didn't feel like talking with Ted Murskey or anyone else. Getting through the day was about all I could handle. Dad hadn't come home at all the night before and still wasn't there when I left for school. I was so worried about what would happen to us, nothing else mattered.

But Ted didn't take the hint. "And," he whispered, "I noticed how people have been ignoring you — except for Mary Chang, of course." His cheeks glowed at the mention of her name.

I stared at him. He'd never seemed interested in girls at all. I thought, Fat chance, guy, so long as Marty's on the scene.

Then what he'd just said registered. He was right. I hadn't talked to anyone on the bus that morning, and no one had come over to me or passed a note my way during French or algebra, or between periods. I guessed I hadn't noticed because, actually, I'd been hoping they'd all leave me alone and keep busy with their new gossip, whatever it might be. Suddenly I knew why I'd been left out of it.

"It's not kind of them to do that," Ted continued softly, and his eyes flashed briefly in Frankel's direction. Ted had never been the target of Frankel Fiction. He aced every test, but never asked questions, never volunteered answers, or did anything remotely likely to call attention to himself. All Frankel had to do was stand within six feet of Ted Murskey and I was sure the poor guy would wet his pants. But, for the moment, he seemed determined to finish what was on his mind.

I observed him through the blue flame. "Not kind to do what, Ted? Not talk to me?" I knew what, but for some reason had to hear him say it.

"To say things . . . behind your back." He shrugged.

The heat rose from inside and burned fiercely through my cheeks. I leaned away from the Bunsen burner, as if the flame must be doing it.

"So" — my voice was shaking and I fanned the air with my hand — "what are they saying about me?" I smiled a little, as if it didn't matter, anyway, and he might as well tell me so we could both have a good laugh.

"About your old man." He paused. "They say he's an addict. That he's probably selling stuff, too."

I fussed with the water spigots, turning them on and off as if testing to see they still worked. "That's a lie," I told him in a nice, even tone.

"Sure." He shrugged.

"It *is*," I said more firmly.

"Look" — he held up both hands — "I don't listen to gossip. But somebody — don't ask me who — saw a man who looked like your father freaking out in the middle of Schennecosett Road, near the Seven-Eleven." He was embarrassed now and avoided my eyes. "They must have mistaken him for your father."

One black thought shot through my mind. Michelle Vonnegut. She *had* to be the one who started the rumor. Her father had seen Dad fall. And he'd walked away without helping. He'd told Michelle, and she probably felt pretty important knowing — or thinking she knew — something no one else knew. But of course she could only take advantage of her news by passing it around.

If I came face to face with her, I'd wring her neck!

But now Ted had lost Frankel. He was desperately scanning the room.

"People make mistakes," I murmured, peering intently at the sheet of litmus, which, not surprisingly, was doing nothing. I'd managed to look terrifically busy while accomplishing zippo after lighting the jet.

"Indeed they do, Miss Monroe," rumbled a deep voice that sent chills clear to my toes.

Ted and I looked up at the exact same moment. Ted turned pale.

"Mr. Murskey," began Frankel, circling from behind Ted's stool, "how is it your burner is still cold? Perhaps you'd like the lovely Miss Monroe to assist you in lighting your fire?"

The room exploded with laughter while poor Ted shriveled up on his stool.

Someday a chem student will have a coronary right in the middle of lab. Then the school board will find out about Frankel.

I COULDN'T GET MICHELLE VONNEGUT OFF MY MIND. It was the dirtiest thing anyone had ever done to me. But if she'd just spread rumors about me, I wouldn't have minded so much. She was hurting Marsha and Dad. Who knows, maybe when Chrissy started school the other little kids wouldn't be allowed to play with him because their parents thought something was wrong with his father.

I didn't see Michelle all day though. I suppose she was avoiding me. So I tried not to think about her and to concentrate on finding a solution to our problems. Once I got home I took the phone book upstairs and spent over an hour in the Yellow Pages.

There are crisis hotlines if you're raped, beaten (by spouse, parent, or absolute stranger — all different numbers), neglected, hungry, drunk, depressed, or want to hear a verse from the Bible. I couldn't find a number for people who aren't absolutely sure what their problem is. Apparently, you have to know what's wrong with you before anyone can help. There was no number for veterans to call.

I did find something called County Resource. But I decided not to call from home. Dad hadn't been around that morning and wasn't now. But he might show up at any time.

After Marsha and Chrissy walked down to the corner to mail a letter, I took the newspaper clipping from Dad's drawer, along with a few papers stamped with Department of Defense seals, and tucked them into my purse. If someone asked for dates or anything, I wanted to be prepared.

The phone rang before I was out the door.

"Josephine Monroe, please," said a businesslike voice. Sanville, my boss.

I could think of only one reason Sanville would call, and that made me feel even more miserable.

"One of my regular waitresses just rang in sick," he said briskly. "You had Friday off, Josephine. How about covering for her?"

I don't have to do this, I thought. If I tell him no, all he can do is brood about it and maybe short me on the schedule for the next few weeks.

But suddenly the hours and the money that came with them seemed more important than before. I felt as if I *had* to have cash on hand — to use, if necessary, or just to hold on to like Linus and his security blanket. Me and my pocket change.

"I'll come," I agreed, then spun around in time to see the front door swing open.

"Who was that?" asked Marsha, seeing the receiver still in my hand.

Chrissy was carrying the mail inside. He sat down with a plop on the carpet and started ripping open envelopes. Marsha performed a sleight of hand that would make a magician look like a klutz. Sweeping away the bills, she left the kid with a batch of store coupons.

"You can have the money," she told him.

He glowed. "Moneys — moneys — moneys — " he chanted like a crazed toddler Midas, pulling out the bright, glossy slips of paper marked "25 cents off" or "$1.00 mail-in rebate."

He actually thinks you can buy stuff with them. When he sees a picture of something he likes, he'll stick the coupon in Marsha's purse, expecting she'll just pick it up on her next trip to the store. His favorite is toilet paper, the kind with the baby on it. I guess he thinks we'll buy him a clone, or a girlfriend maybe. Who knows.

Marsha straightened up and looked at me thoughtfully. I intentionally turned away and walked into the kitchen.

My head had buzzed as if it were full of wet bees all

day. And every time I looked at food my stomach sent little signals to my brain. "Don't bother sending any of that down, you hear?" it threatened. " 'Cause you'll be real sorry."

Taking out the milk and a jar of honey, I measured some of both into the blender. One mostly brown banana was left on the counter. The insides were okay, so I sliced it into the glass container. I figured: make a shake. Keep it simple and the stomach might not notice.

"Sanville," I called out a long time after her question. "He needs me to work tonight."

I could tell from her silence that she was making up her mind about something. I didn't turn to check out her expression. Seeing her look so tired and confused made me feel worse.

"I haven't told you something very important," she began.

I held my breath. Maybe she'd finally taken Dad's problem seriously. If she took charge even now, I could quit worrying about all of us. I wished so hard for that to happen.

"I want you to know I appreciate what you're doing, Josie. I haven't asked you to help me. But you've cleaned the house and bought food with your own money. I want you to know I'll pay you back as soon as I get my first paycheck. And I'm glad you're not seeing Brian. I know that's hard on you, but I think it'll help make life easier for us."

For you, maybe, I thought. I was so disappointed that I couldn't even look at her.

After I'd forced down the first two swallows of milk shake, Chrissy made a beeline for the glass. I boosted him into my lap and helped him drink a little. When

101

he won't eat for Marsha she always makes him something like this, with a raw egg and wheat germ in it. Then I pretend it's a special treat for me, and he can't have any. Works every time.

Watching his fat fingers curl around my glass as he gulped, I kissed the top of his head.

"Anyway," Marsha blurted on, sorting through the mail, "you're doing a lot to help."

"But it's not enough," I said over the lump in my throat.

Marsha peered up at the clock and rubbed her eyes that were suddenly almost as red as her hair. "Look, I can't let you have the car tonight because I need it myself. But I'll drive you to Harvey's, and we'll have a nice girl talk on the way," she offered with forced cheerfulness. "I have a wonderful idea about how to redecorate your room, and it will cost almost nothing."

No way did I want to chat about wallpaper and curtains! There simply wasn't a lot to say to her, unless it was about Dad. And she'd obviously decided to avoid that subject. So, I was going to have to handle this on my own. And if I told her what I was planning to do, she'd make me promise not to.

"That's okay," I said. "Mary's driving tonight."

I left Chrissy in my chair, polishing off the shake.

After I'd changed I ran across the backyards to Mary's house, trying to decide how to get to work if she was the one who'd called in sick.

# CHAPTER FOURTEEN

"WATCH OUT!" GUS SCOWLED DOWN ON ME. "WHERE you got your head, girl?" he demanded. "Touch that grill, the heat'll pull the skin straight off your hand!"

I stared at the steaming iron surface. "Sorry, Gus," I mumbled, and backed away meekly.

I hadn't been able to stop thinking about Michelle. When we were in elementary school, before Mary's family had moved to Groton, Michelle and I had been good friends. By the time we'd hit high school, though, we saw each other only in the halls and at a party now and then. I was recommended for honors level courses; she skated through midlevels. Although we both knew she was smart enough to hack honors, she didn't want to have to work too hard. She loved being able to join drama, yearbook, cheerleaders, anything prestigious that put her in with the "right" crowd — Pointers.

I didn't blame her for wanting to be accepted. Sometimes I'd envied her. And, in our freshman year, she'd made a game of introducing me to her new friends. I suppose it made her feel superior. Some of them were nice, but they expected you to come to every party (and there was one every Friday and Saturday) and to spend all afternoon at one or another club meeting at school. Then they'd go out to eat in a group and often meet at someone's house to do homework. It was rough keeping up with them, and my grades that first year weren't very good at all. Part of the reason I took the job at Harvey's was to give me an excuse to break away from them. But I'd always suspected Michelle knew and resented the fact that I was rejecting her crowd. Maybe she took it personally, although I hadn't intended to hurt her.

So I hadn't been thinking about what I was doing when I set the tray down too near the hot cast iron where the burgers sizzled and spit.

As pooped and preoccupied as I was with Michelle's

betrayal, if Gus hadn't been there to stop me I might have stretched out on the grill without feeling a thing. My ears rang, my eyeballs ached. The long muscles in the backs of my legs cramped.

I'd tried to clear my head with a cup of coffee when I'd first come in to work. I needed to make some important decisions. Dad hadn't been home since his fight with Marsha last night. Sometimes I worried that he wouldn't come back at all, even though that's what I'd wished at first. Then I'd start trembling and my hand would slip off the heavy ceramic plates, because it was so awful imagining what it would be like never to see him again. Maybe he'd collapsed in a road again and someone driving a car hadn't seen him! Maybe he'd completely lost touch with who he was and where he was, and would never snap out of it.

And stupid Michelle was making everything worse with her gossip.

A crowd of girls came in at nine o'clock, jingling the bells that hung from a spring over Harvey's door. They giggled and consulted for a minute — counter or booth — then chose stools at the long white counter. Michelle, Tori, and two others from their crowd — the Swanson twins. As soon as I realized who it was, I turned my back on them and started collecting sugar dispensers from each of the tables.

When I took the filled ones back fifteen minutes later, the four girls' eyes followed me. Let them sit, I thought, hoping they'd get up and leave. But a minute later Sanville walked over and stood behind me.

"How long have those customers been waiting?" he asked.

I wiped the stainless-steel shelf with a damp cloth, making sure I got every spilled sugar grain, looking super efficient. "I think they just came in."

He waited without moving. I rinsed out the cloth and wiped down the whole surface again.

"You can finish that later, Josephine," he said irritably. "Go wait on them."

They grew quiet when I approached; Michelle studied the menu, keeping her eyes down so she wouldn't have to meet mine. Nevertheless, a tiny twist lifted one corner of her mouth. And Tori and the Swansons were struggling to hide smiles, so I knew they'd been talking about me.

I smiled politely for Sanville's benefit, but the rage in me kept building. Was it fair that they treated my family as if we were a joke? And suddenly I guessed that they'd come in on purpose, curious to see how the rumors were affecting me. Maybe wanting to find out if I even knew I was being talked about. That would be funniest of all — if I just hadn't caught on.

Satisfied that everything seemed in order now, Sanville disappeared past the rest rooms and into his closet-size office.

"Sl-l-l-ime," I hissed, my voice so low only they could hear.

Looking over the top of the glossy plastic, Michelle sat up straight, her eyes wide with surprise. She obviously hadn't expected me to know she was the one behind the talk, and certainly didn't anticipate a confrontation. She opened her mouth to protest, but I slammed the order pad on the counter in front of her and she closed her mouth.

"You were so damn concerned, weren't you?" I sneered. "So concerned that you had to shoot off your mouth to the whole world! You know absolutely nothing about my family!"

Michelle laughed nervously. One of the twins touched her on the arm and glanced meaningfully out the high windows, toward the parking lot glowing under mercury vapor lamps.

"Right! Get out!" I shouted, almost losing control.

Conversation at the nearby booths ceased abruptly. I could feel people watching me, but that no longer mattered.

"Josie, I — " began Michelle.

"Does spreading lies about people make you feel important?" I demanded.

Everything around us seemed to be in darkness. There was only Michelle at the end of a long, dark tunnel in front of me. She teetered on her stool, smiling lopsidedly, her eyes worried.

Distant bells tinkled as somebody came or left the restaurant. Neither of us looked to see who it was.

At last Michelle found her voice. "We came in here for dinner," she said with dignity, a stubborn expression clinging to her face. "Why don't you let someone else wait on us, Josie."

"It can't be easy," somebody commented in a sickly, sympathetic tone. One of the Swansons, I supposed vaguely.

The warning drumroll in my ears turned into a roar. All the resentment and fear and shame boiled up inside me and came frothing out.

"He's not what you think! Liar! Little sneaky tramp of a liar!"

Tears streamed hot and stinging down my cheeks. I lunged across the counter, going for Michelle. Two fistfuls of pink angora vest came up in my hands. I was shaking her, side to side, and she slipped off the stool but I still held on. She grabbed at my hair, screeching and pulling, making tears come faster to my already swollen eyes. I could no longer see anything but a red blur of frantic movement. People hastily moved away from us, leaving the restaurant or forming a circle to watch from a safe distance.

But Mary was somewhere in the background pleading. "Let her go, Josie. Oh, my, gosh! Oh, no, Sanville will *kill* you!"

"I'll kill *her*!" I screamed again and again.

Michelle clawed desperately at my face. I gripped all the tighter, banging her chin down against the hard plastic ledge between us. Then somebody was vaulting over the counter, reaching around my shoulders from behind, prying my fingers out of matted pink fuzz.

"Make her stop, Brian!" cried Mary. "Get her out of here — "

"What the hell!" Sanville was running down the aisle between the two rows of booths.

By now Brian had pinned me against his chest. The fury inside me subsided almost instantly, and all I could do was to sob hysterically into his sweater.

"What the hell is going on?" demanded Sanville.

"Beats me," replied Gus in his solemn bass.

"Can't you kids keep your love lives out of my restaurant?" Sanville stared at Michelle, who was holding her chin in one hand as if it might fall off any minute. Her vest was pulled out of shape and bulged six inches lower on one side. "Are you all right, missy? Gus, get this girl some ice. Are you sure you're all right?"

Michelle kept nodding, while her jaw swelled. Her eyes never left me.

"I'm fine," she said, backing toward the door.

The other girls clustered around her like a secret service squad protecting the president.

Tori wrapped Michelle in a comforting arm. As they escaped through the door, she threw me a look of disgust. "You really know how to treat friends, Monroe."

There was a long silence after they'd left.

"I don't even want to know what that was about," said Sanville at last, his hands twitching at his sides.

I kept my face buried in Brian's shoulder.

Sanville cleared his throat. "Hey, look. I'll punch out your time card. You go home and . . . work this out." He started to walk away. "You're usually such a dependable kid, Josephine. Don't do this to me again, huh?"

"I — I can't go home," I said before he'd reached the time clock on the back wall. "Mary drove me."

He turned and glanced from Mary to me, then to Brian. "So, what's the big deal? Your boyfriend here will drive you — that's what you wanted anyway. Isn't it?"

"I — I need the money." The words came out in a long, weak sigh.

Sanville looked surprised, as if there might be more to this than he'd at first suspected. "All right," he agreed at last. "Stay then. But take ten minutes to get yourself together, your . . . your face," he gestured uncertainly. "Wash up, maybe go outside and get some air. And when you come back, no more of these wrestling matches. Damn barroom brawl," he muttered, turning away. "Sorry," he called to the customers who remained. "Everything is fine now. Sorry about that."

"Oh, Brian," I moaned.

He leaned away a little and touched my face gently. "She scratched you up pretty bad." I could feel the white-hot welts still rising.

Mary brought a wet paper towel and handed it to

108

Brian. "I'm sorry, Josie. I didn't see her come in. I'd have taken your station."

I nodded to show I understood. I really didn't think I could speak over the raw fire in my throat. And I didn't want to cry anymore in front of everyone.

Brian patted my cheeks with the dripping towel. "Come on," he said quietly, and squeezed my waist. "Outside."

I LEANED AGAINST THE BRICK WALL OF THE FIRST NATIONAL. The chill air on my face did make it feel better. I looked up at the stars — millions of them. Other people had stood under those stars a hundred years ago, a thousand, five thousand. Some nights they'd made love. Others, they'd killed an enemy.

"Josie," Brian whispered. "It's gotten worse. Hasn't it?"

I nodded.

"Why does he hate me so much?"

I reached up to touch the soft brown hairs in front of his ear, and smiled through the glaze of tears still fogging my vision. "I don't know how anyone could hate you." I rose on tiptoe and kissed him on the lips.

"This is rotten. I can't stand staying away from you, Josie. Can't I even call to talk to you?"

"Better if you don't."

"Fantastic. How long will this go on, anyway?"

I took the newspaper clipping and Defense Department papers out of my purse and handed them to him.

He held the article at an angle to the street lamp. "What's this?"

"Read," I told him. "My dad was in Vietnam."

He looked at me for a second, then down at the newspaper in his hand. "That's about two decades ago.

He hasn't acted like this before, has he? At least, you never said anything about it."

"No." I took a deep breath. "I think maybe he's been holding it inside for a long time. But now he can't help what he's feeling."

He finished reading the article, glanced quickly at each of the other papers, then looked down at me with a serious expression.

"Josie, you're not going to like this. But I think you don't have any choice." He hesitated. "You're going to have to talk to the police."

"No!" I backed away.

"Now, Josie, listen." He grabbed my arm and pulled me back against the building. "Marsha's not helping him; you admitted that. Meanwhile, he gets worse every time he freaks out. And Mary —"

I pushed him away. "How do you know about Mary?"

He looked embarrassed. "I wasn't supposed to say anything about that."

"She called you," I guessed.

"Yeah. But, now, Josie, don't be mad at her. Your father really scared her. And her parents. Apparently he's been prowling around the neighborhood. Her father has seen him in their yard several times. The Changs are convinced he's dangerously unstable. Seeing this article makes me think they may be right. That's why I came to Harvey's tonight. The more I thought about you being alone with him, the worse I felt about it. What if he takes after you when Marsha isn't there to stop him?"

"He'd never hurt me," I said quickly.

"Josie" — he hugged me, hard — "you don't know that. He's sick; he needs help."

"But not the police," I said firmly. "And if you tell your father about any of this . . . I'll never speak to you as long as I live. I swear, Brian Pedersen."

He thought for a minute. "All right. I'll help however you want. Just don't shut me out, Josie."

His arms came around me and held on. I pressed against his body and felt a little of the tension ease off. From now on I'd handle this my way.

# CHAPTER FIFTEEN

GROTON HIGH SCHOOL EMPLOYS THREE SCHOLASTIC counselors. Jarrett King gets *I* through *P*.

I sat in the lime-green outer office for ten minutes before a secretary opened the door and waved me inside.

"Hey there, Josie!" Jarrett flashed me a big grin across his desk. "How's life?"

Jarrett — he insists that all the students call him by his first name — played tennis for UCLA. He looks like a young Robert Redford with sun-streaked blond hair, a tight gut under his surfer's jersey, and long brown arms that stay tanned all through the winter — in Connecticut, no less.

"Fine, Mr. King," I said, and sat in the chair opposite him.

"Jarrett," he told me, and smiled sunnily again.

"Jarrett," I repeated, and looked down at my hands.

He waited a moment before going on. "Since everything's cool," he began at last, watching my face, "you must have wondered why I called you out of fifth period."

I inclined my head to one side and half smiled, as if just mildly curious.

He looked down at a page of notes on his desk. "Several of your teachers have expressed concern with your work in the past few weeks. Generally a few days' falling off doesn't show up in our records or affect your overall grade. But you've always been so consistent, Josie. A strong student really. And I guess they're afraid that if this trend, or whatever it is, continues, you may not pass the quarter."

I looked at him, honestly surprised. "I — I didn't think it was that bad."

He opened a buff cardboard file that was under his notes. "You pulled a sixty-one on a major French test. You have work missing in algebra, lit, and chemistry. Those assignments presently stand as zeros." He shut the folder and studied me while he spoke. "I ran an informal survey this morning, after receiving deficiency notices to pass through to you from two of your teachers. The rest agree: Your attitude in class has changed radically. That's what they're most concerned with."

"Oh," I said.

He picked up two yellow pencils that had never been sharpened and drumrolled the eraser ends on his blotter. "I thought, possibly, you'd like to talk about it."

"What?" I played stupid.

He waved one pencil in the air. "Whatever is bothering you."

"Nothing in particular," I said. "I guess I just wasn't aware how much I'd been goofing off."

"Have you been ill? If so, that's a legitimate excuse. A makeup schedule can be arranged."

I shook my head.

He coughed once and dropped the pencils into a juice can decorated with crayon flowers that spelled out "Daddy." I'd never thought of him as having kids. I hadn't even known that he was married.

"I also notice," he started again, "that you work twenty hours or more every week. As a waitress?"

I shifted my glance away from the can, aware that he was trying to make a point but not quite sure where he was headed. "Yes," I answered warily.

"That's demanding work, energy-wise, time-wise. Perhaps the best thing to do would be eliminate as many of your outside activities as possible, including your job."

"No," I said firmly. "I'm not quitting my job."

"I didn't say you had to, permanently. Just for a while, a month or so, to let you concentrate on your studies." When I didn't answer he continued anyway. "You realize that, if necessary, we can request your parents to inform your employer you no longer have their permission to work."

I sank in the seat, feeling hollow inside. "I can handle it," I told him grimly. "You don't have to do that." I couldn't say that I needed the money, really *needed* it. In fact, it probably wouldn't be enough as it was. Marsha couldn't possibly be making much more than minimum wage. And if Dad didn't sell houses, he didn't get paid.

We sat for several minutes in silence. Jarrett didn't dismiss me. And I didn't offer any explanation.

"Josie," he said at last, "are there problems at home? Anything you can't deal with . . ."

I shook my head, hard, and realized as his eyes narrowed that this was the first time he'd seen the bad side of my face. The marks from Michelle's nails were still pretty fresh. I quickly looked off to one side.

"I'm here for that, too. Or, I can arrange for you to have time with the school psychologist next Tuesday. Sooner, if you'd like."

I drew back my shoulders, smiled across the desk at him, and gave a great imitation of a lighthearted laugh. "I'll bring up my grades by the end of the marking period, Jarrett," I promised, standing up. "Honest."

I slipped my purse strap over one shoulder and walked straight out through the office. I didn't look back to see if he was convinced.


DURING LUNCH I CALLED BRIAN. HE WORKED IN HIS school's health room one day a week, and I caught him there.

"You might have asked your counselor what to do," he said when I told him about Mr. King — Jarrett.

I didn't think that was such a good idea. "He knows about GPAs and SATs. I doubt if he'd know anything about jungle warfare."

"He might at least be able to tell you where to go for help."

"Well, it doesn't matter anyhow," I said. "I think I've found a number to call. The Community Resource operator gave me a place in New Haven."

The cafeteria was packed and noisy. I had to shout into the phone and hold one hand over my free ear in order to hear Brian.

"What kind of place?" he asked.

"A vet counseling center and — "

"Get a move on," the guy behind me muttered impatiently.

"Sorry," I apologized, "this is kind of important."

"Yeah, sure." He snickered and shook his head.

"In New Haven?" asked Brian. "I don't know, Josie. How would you get your dad to go there?"

"I'll find a way." Once I find him, I added silently.

"Are you going to call now?"

"I can't. Too many people." The guy waiting for the phone was standing so that his arm was brushing against my shoulder blade — just to hurry me along. I tried to ignore him. "But I don't want to do it from home. So I'll probably wait until the middle of the afternoon, and — "

The bell rang, the commotion instantly tripled, and the guy with his elbow in my back started swearing.

"I gotta go!" I shouted into the receiver.

"Can I call you tonight?" Brian asked quickly.

My heart took a tender little leap. I smiled, then sighed. "You'd better not."

FRENCH WAS LAST PERIOD FOR ME THAT DAY. I SKIPPED it and returned to the cafeteria. A few kids were getting stuff out of the vending machines, otherwise the place was ghost city.

A receptionist answered in New Haven; she said Dr. Whitehead was on another line. Would I care to leave my number?

I chewed my bottom lip, trying to think fast. Obviously, I couldn't leave the school's number, either the office or the pay phone. And if someone at the vet center called at home and I wasn't there . . . If Marsha or Dad answered . . . Marsha would be furious, and there was no telling what Dad would think — or do.

"No," I said abruptly. "I'll call back." But I knew that might not be easy.

# CHAPTER SIXTEEN

WHEN I GOT HOME FROM SCHOOL, I FELT LIKE SLEEPING for a week straight, although it was only the middle of the afternoon. It was the second day since Dad had disappeared. I hadn't slept much nights. When I did sleep, it wasn't deep. I'd wake at the least sound, wondering if it was him, unsure what sort of mood he'd be in. I was afraid he would come back, then afraid I'd never see him again. I couldn't decide which was worse.

Marsha had refused to call the police to ask about filing a missing person's report. "He just needs some time," she'd say whenever I asked. I began to wonder if she might be relieved to have him gone, and that made me feel terrible.

A note on the fridge from Marsha asked me to take the car and run errands for her. Chrissy was at Mrs. Bedloe's around the corner. I had to pick him up at five.

After taking the Browning from its cabinet in the den, I zipped it into my carrying case and put it in the car. I got my paycheck first, and added that to the little bit of money Marsha had left. I bought everything on her list at the Stop & Shop, passed up the Twinkies after considerable debate, and picked up extra cans of soup and tuna fish and a box of powdered milk.

In the parking lot I hefted the bags from the steel cart into the trunk with my gun. And instead of going straight home, I drove north to Riveredge.

I used the pay phone on the outside wall of the scorer's shed. This time the receptionist recognized my voice.

"Don't hang up, dear," she told me gently. "Dr. Whitehead will be right with you."

Dr. Whitehead — I somehow pictured an albino rat with bright pink eyes, a stethoscope hung around his neck — had an ageless voice. "How can I help you, young lady?"

All of a sudden my voice wouldn't work. Coiling the phone cord around one finger, I finally managed to whisper, "I'm scared."

There was a very short silence from Dr. Whitehead's side. "What's frightening you?" he asked seriously, as if he didn't doubt for a minute I was telling the truth.

At first I couldn't think how to start. But once I got going it didn't seem so hard to talk. After all, he didn't know who or where I was. From fifty miles away I felt pretty safe. I wasn't having my father committed or anything. I was just getting advice. So, even if I did slip and say something that might make trouble for Dad, this Whitehead wouldn't know how to find us. I know about tracing calls, but I don't think people like doctors do that. No one would trust them anymore.

I told him about what had happened outside the 7-Eleven, and about the hole in the wall and the ashtray throwing and about the newspaper article Dad had kept. I didn't tell him the part about Dad almost belting me. We talked for twenty minutes, and I had to put in extra coins five different times. He wanted dates and the names of places my father had been stationed in Vietnam, and for how long. I read aloud what I could find in Dad's papers: "Tan Son Nhut — June 1, 1969." Then more places, more dates. He'd taken two consecutive tours of duty, it turned out, and was there for two whole years.

"Do you suppose he would come to see me?" asked

Whitehead when I'd told him everything I could.

My heart bumped, almost happily. If this man wanted to see Dad, didn't it mean for sure that he could help him? Didn't that *prove* there was a reason connected to the war for everything Dad had been doing?

I had visions of my father, Jack Monroe, in battle gear. Bombs exploding to his right, his left. Scrambling on hands and knees to a wounded soldier. Ignoring his own danger, he'd comfort the other man — maybe just eighteen or nineteen, not much older than me — then hoist him on to his shoulder and dash amid enemy fire to safety. He was a hero! It was the men he couldn't save who haunted him now.

"Then you think he's . . . that he's definitely doing all this because of what happened to him in Asia?" I asked.

"I can't say for certain," he explained cautiously, the way doctors do when they're not talking to other doctors. "From what you've told me, he's experiencing flashbacks — snatches of time from the past that he mentally replays. Something frightening or troubling that happened to him."

"But Vietnam was so long ago, and he seemed perfectly normal until just recently."

"Yes." He sounded puzzled. "Your father's problems do sound unusual in that way. Most men would have shown signs of being unable to cope with their experience much sooner. If it is his memory of the war that's causing him to act as he is, something must have disturbed the tricky mental balance he'd been managing to keep for so long. Something set him off."

I thought about that. "How would you find out what his problem is for sure?"

118

"I'd need to interview him. Perhaps discuss what occurred during those two years a number of times before I could understand the root of his problem."

My heart wobbled and sank. "He never mentions the army. I don't know if he'll agree to see you." I chewed one nail nervously. "I guess it must hurt to think about that time. Wouldn't it be even harder to talk about? Especially to a stranger?"

"That's a large part of many men's problems," said Whitehead. "They don't believe anyone who wasn't there can possibly understand what they went through. And, in many ways, they're right. Most people become uncomfortable hearing about the horrible things that happened; they're embarrassed. Others find killing for any reason morally repugnant, even though these men were doing the job their government sent them to do."

"There have been other wars."

"You're right. Vietnam was nothing new in many ways. But the men, women, too, were treated differently than in previous wars. Instead of being shipped out with the group you trained with, many were detailed on an individual basis. You were on your own going over there. You tried not to become too close emotionally to any of the people there because your buddy might get blown up that afternoon. And, when you came home, it was in your own time." If you came home at all, I thought sadly. "You'd probably never see the men you left behind again. Sometimes you felt as if you were deserting them — leaving them to keep on fighting while you went home."

"Maybe that's why my father went back for a second tour?" I asked.

"Maybe so. I was in the air force and served in Asia

during the war. I wasn't involved in hand-to-hand combat. But, when I came home, I still felt as if I'd left my job undone."

"*You* were there, Dr. Whitehead?" I asked quietly. For some reason, that meant a lot to me.

"Yes," he said evenly. "I was."

"But you're . . . all right?"

He laughed, and I liked the mellow, soothing sound of his voice. "If you mean, do I bust chairs over people's heads and lose days on end out of my life," he said, as if he was trying hard to make a joke of it, "no. But I remember a lot. And there are nights I don't sleep at all."

"I don't think my dad sleeps." I suppose I'd known that for some time now, but suddenly everything seemed clearer.

"I wouldn't be surprised," he said softly.

I thought about all we'd said, half-listening to the background interference of another call breaking across our line.

"The important thing," he continued after a while, "is for him to get help. But he'll have to come in voluntarily."

My stomach sank with a thud. I wanted this to be over. Maybe, on second thought, getting him committed to a hospital wasn't such a bad idea. I wanted someone to take this man away and bring back my dad — the old one who used to race me on bicycle to Dairy Queen every Saturday, or chew me out when I let my shoulder drop at shooting practice, or make lunch in a brown paper sack for school when I was too little to do it and before Marsha came.

"If — " I said slowly, "if I can talk him into coming, what will happen?"

"He'll have an opportunity to speak with men who've had similar experiences to his. They'll help one another cope with the reality of what they went through. It's partly that, you know, shutting out things, denying them. He can't talk about it because he doesn't want to admit it ever happened."

"Whatever *did* happen," I whispered, "must have been awful."

I thought I heard a pencil scratching softly on paper, but it didn't particularly bother me that he was taking notes.

"Are you afraid of finding out what happened to your father?" he asked.

I hadn't thought about that. But it probably had been at the back of my mind for some time.

"What if he . . ." I choked a little and looked around to make sure, absolutely sure, nobody was listening. "I mean, in school we read about some things — My Lai. American soldiers killing a whole village of people. Women, little kids, old people. What if my father . . ."

His voice seeped soothingly, like honey, into the receiver and I pressed my ear closer to it, needing to hear that and nothing else.

"It's so unlikely," he said. "Most probably he saw men dying, boys who were homesick and scared and miserable, people doing what they had to do just to survive — whether they were U.S. servicemen like himself or Vietnamese. You don't forget that sort of waste and pain."

I nodded, although he couldn't see me.

"If you feel threatened though," he continued, "if he comes home and keeps up like this or gets worse, you'll have to go to the police. If he won't do anything for himself, you'll have to do it for him."

"I can't do that!" I cried. "There must be some other way. There *is*!"

He sighed. "Don't wait too long," he warned. Then, "I have an idea. What say I send you some literature? Knowing some of what your dad may be going through might help you and your mother deal with him until he'll ask for help."

"I'd like that," I told him. "But I don't . . ."

He waited for me to go on, and when I didn't he suggested, "I can send a package to a library near where you live. You tell me which one. They'll already have copies of some of this, but they can hold these especially for you to pick up." He hesitated. "I'll put any name on the package you like; just ask the reference librarian for the material after about five days."

"Like a code name," I thought aloud.

"Any one you choose."

Even though I really did trust him, I liked his suggestion. I asked, "You know Napoleon?"

He chuckled. "The emperor? Short dude with his hand in his jacket?"

I smiled. "That one. His queen was Josephine."

"An elegant lady, and very intelligent. The emperor valued her tact and sound political advice, even after he divorced her for not giving him a son."

"I know," I said.

"I expect you're very much alike — Josephine."


I SHOT ONE ROUND BEFORE LEAVING RIVEREDGE, BUT DID incredibly lousy. I couldn't keep my mind on the traps as they zipped across the gray sky. I thought, no one uses their own name for a code. Never mind. Nobody's ever going to know it's me. I hope.

122

# CHAPTER SEVENTEEN

I LOCKED THE BROWNING IN THE DEN CABINET DOWN-stairs, then jumping up, slid the key on top, way behind the carved maple finials and out of Chrissy's reach — even if he stood on a chair.

When I picked him up at Mrs. Bedloe's he looked beat. Mrs. Bedloe watched at least five toddlers for neighborhood mothers, and Chrissy wasn't used to playing for so long with other kids.

Poor kid, he must really miss Marsha.

I let him have two Oreos to munch in his crib while he rested before supper. He'd make a mess but at least he'd be happy, and I could wash the sheets later.

I hung my jacket in the living room closet. As I hooked the wire hanger over the rod a couple of coins fell and rolled across the carpet. I chased them down and, when I felt inside the pocket, found a hole in the lining.

Chrissy had dozed off upstairs, and I was sitting at the kitchen table, trying to mend the tear, when Dad's car pulled into the driveway. I concentrated on making smaller, neater stitches. He'd been gone for days — with no explanation. What was I supposed to say to him now? But he went straight upstairs without setting foot in the kitchen. And I heard the shower turn on.

Ten minutes later, while I was still struggling with the hole and trying to decide what to do when he came down, he walked in.

"Afternoon, missy," he chirped, and cuffed me play-fully on the ear.

I dropped the needle in surprise and stared at the

back of his head as he poured himself a tall glass of cold orange juice. He picked up the Hartford *Courant* that Marsha had left unread on the kitchen table. A second later I heard the creak of his recliner as he settled back with his newspaper.

I stopped breathing. What was he up to? I waited, wondering if I should stay where I was or go upstairs, my stomach tightening because it didn't know what to expect. I picked up the spool of thread and needle, then pushed away from the table and leaned around the living room doorway.

He'd folded the sports section in half and was reading. Several days' growth of beard shadowed his face. Otherwise he looked clean and comfortable and relaxed.

"Homecoming game in two weeks," he said, without looking up.

He was acting almost normal! But somehow that made me no less nervous.

"That's right," I said, as if I couldn't wait, although games and parties were the farthest things from my mind these days. And I realized right then how totally different my life had become. There seemed to be nothing I could depend upon anymore, except maybe Brian.

"Going?"

"Huh?"

"Are you going to the game between Groton and New London?"

"Guess so." I punched the needle through the paper top of the spool a couple times. "I don't know."

"Chrissy's almost old enough to enjoy that sort of thing. Don't you think?"

I got up slowly, crossed the living room, and sat on the very front edge of the middle cushion on the sofa.

I guess Chrissy might like it," I agreed cautiously. "He wouldn't really know what was going on, the game and score and all. But he might get a charge out of the shouting and streamers. And he adores hot dogs." I smiled to myself. "I bet he'd go crazy over one of those little plastic megaphones the student council sells."

Dad lowered the paper and leaned his head back against the leather pillow. He watched me from under lowered lids. His eyes were a thin gray blue and lazy, and the muscles around his mouth were, for once, at ease.

"Why don't we plan on going, you and I?" he said with a laid-back smile. "If Marsha thinks Chrissy can handle it and she'd enjoy coming along, we'll make a day of it. The whole family."

"Really?" I cried, grinning so hard my jaw hurt. This was almost too good to be true. I stopped grinning. This *was* too good to be true.

He glanced up from the newspaper and winked. "Why not? I'll bet everyone would have a great time. Then we'll come home to a big turkey dinner with all the trimmings. Of course," he interrupted himself, his spirits visibly dimming, "that would mean Marsha would have to be up awfully early to put in the bird."

"No, she won't," I insisted, unwilling to let his plan fizzle. Even if I didn't believe he was back to his old self, I couldn't resist the chance to remind him of how we used to be. A family holiday sounded like the perfect way to do that. "If she wants to sleep in, I'll start Thanksgiving dinner. I know how to stuff a turkey. It's not hard at all."

"How do you stuff a turkey?" he asked.

"Feed him a ten-course meal, then take away his Alka-Seltzer," I said with a straight face.

"Oh," he groaned. "That's bad. That's criminal."

"Really," I agreed, laughing.

Suddenly, he looked at me with a solemn expression. Clearing his throat, he announced casually, "Guess who sold a house today?" Immediately he looked down again at his paper. But a smile tugged at the corners of his mouth.

"You?" Clutching my heart, I gasped in fake shock.

"Two hundred thousand," he said through the newsprint. I heard the pride in his voice. "One of the beach houses down on Long Point."

"Is that right?" I was nodding, showing him I was moderately impressed. But, inside, I was laughing, shouting with relief, doing cartwheels. I just didn't want to make too big a deal about it, as if I'd been holding my breath waiting for this moment. If he knew, maybe then he wouldn't feel so good about himself. Had he stayed away on purpose until he made a sale?

"What time is it?" he asked.

"About five-thirty." I stood up, still struggling not to go overboard. "Want me to turn on the news?"

"Sure." Then he added, "Boy, I'm hungry. Any clue what Marsha's planning for dinner?"

I checked in the fridge but nothing had been prepared or was thawing or anything. "Your guess is good as mine," I called from the kitchen. "How about popcorn while we wait?"

"Sounds fine to me," he mumbled from inside his paper.

I poured vegetable oil into the bottom of the electric popper, let it heat, then added a third of a cup of kernels.

The news was on and from what I was hearing it sounded like a tropical storm had hit the eastern coast of Florida. They'd had plenty of warning though. Most everyone had been evacuated.

I thought about Dad's Thanksgiving plans. The only drawback was that Brian wasn't included. And it made me feel sort of rotten to be so happy without him. But we still had time. Maybe next week I could bring up the possibility of Brian coming along to the game.

I found bowls for the popcorn in the cupboard. The announcer was talking about a hundred-million-dollar defense contract that had just been awarded to General Dynamics, the shipyard up river that builds submarines for the navy. A couple of men who work there were being interviewed on camera, and they talked all around the reporter's questions.

I laughed. "What a hoot! No one ever says anything really interesting." I dug in another cupboard for Marsha's special butter-flavored salt. "So why do reporters keep asking the same dumb questions? Is it because they know the answers are classified and they like to sound mysterious?"

Dad chuckled from the living room. "Could be," he said.

I poured myself a glass of diet root beer and Dad a ginger ale because he enjoys flavors that aren't too sweet.

Another story was on when I came around the corner with our glasses on a tray. Something about Vietnam again. I hesitated and looked away from the TV screen toward Dad. But he was deep into his newspaper and didn't seem to notice the old footage they were showing of dense jungle foliage and American soldiers carrying rifles. Their faces tense with concentration, they worked their way cautiously through the vines — checking for the trip wires of booby traps, the announcer explained.

I realized that the story had to do with veterans visiting Vietnam now, returning in peacetime to the same cities and villages where they'd fought twenty years before. Maybe, I thought, that's one way of making yourself believe it's finished.

Then I decided, well, why not? If at least talking about Vietnam would help him, as Dr. Whitehead had said, why not now?

"Umm — the oil is almost hot enough," I announced. "Popcorn will be served in five minutes."

He took the glass of ginger ale I'd brought him, then glanced toward the TV screen. There was no change in his expression.

I took a deep breath. "Did you have to do that in Vietnam?" I asked. "Did you march through jungles and stuff?"

He followed the shaky footage.

"Yes," he said after a while.

I barely breathed the words. "What was it like, Dad?"

His eyes never moved from the screen. But he lifted one shoulder and grimaced slightly. "Nothing to talk about, Josephine. Not worth it, you know. That's all in the past."

I watched him, disturbed by the way he'd tensed up all over and his eyes had become super alert.

Suddenly the popcorn kernels started pinging out in the kitchen. They sounded frantic, as if they were trying to break out of their miniprison. And, with each crack, a tiny muscle twitched at the edge of his mouth.

He ran his tongue along one lip, then the other as he scanned the living room.

"Dad," I said, my voice sounding hoarse. I moved to stand beside his chair, then bent down until my face was directly in what should have been his line of vision. "It's just popcorn!"

Our snack was exploding like crazy out in the kitchen, and the crunching sound on the TV, of men in boots tromping through heavy brush, filled the room. I couldn't tell if he was hearing me at all.

I shut off the TV, then ran out to the kitchen and pulled the plug on the popper. A few last kernels banged, then the house was silent.

"Did that popping sound remind you of gunfire?" I asked, hovering in the kitchen doorway. I was afraid to get too close to him now. "Like outside the Seven-Eleven when the car backfired?"

He didn't answer. His eyes were still fixed on the dark TV screen.

Then, from the stairway, came a tough, puppyish growl. I spun around. Chrissy was crawling down the steps and across the living room carpet, playing Ferocious Tiger. He was also covered with Oreo from head to toe. I lunged forward to intercept him, but he raced me to the recliner. Before I could catch him, he'd pounced up onto Dad's lap and began gnawing on his neck.

Dad's shoulders shook. He looked pale and panicky. Then, with a convulsive movement, he reached out and hugged Chrissy hard to him.

"I won't let them hurt you, son," he sobbed. "They won't get you!"

Chrissy stopped playing and began to whimper, his eyes huge and terrified as they turned to me for help.

# CHAPTER EIGHTEEN

WE SAT ON THE SWING IN THE BACKYARD UNTIL IT GOT dark. Chrissy was getting hungry now and wanted to go inside but I wouldn't let him.

"Don't you want to swing anymore?" I asked. He wriggled out of my lap.

"Oreos!" he demanded with determination, marching toward the back door.

"If Mom thinks you're too hungry to wait for dinner," I called after him, "she'll probably open up a can of beef stew. Why don't we wait out here, Chrissy, so she'll make us something good?"

He paused, thinking about that. Maybe it sounded logical to him.

He always wants his food separated into distinct piles, or else made so he can pull it apart, like peanut butter and bread. Stew confuses him because the sauce sticks to everything, and he can't tell a carrot from a potato. He sits with gravy dripping from his fingers and a look of disgust on his face and doesn't eat much of anything unless Marsha makes him.

But whether or not what I'd told him made sense, I knew I *had* to make him stay away from Dad. Something about that last swing between moods frightened me worse than his silence or bursts of violence had. I'd been forced to pull Chrissy out of Dad's arms. The little kid's lip had been quivering and his cheeks turning red from being squeezed so hard. And Dad hadn't even known he was hurting him!

About ten minutes ago I'd heard Marsha's car pull in, but I'd still stayed out back even though it was dark and my nose was numbing from the cold. I knew she could see us from the kitchen window and wouldn't be worried.

When I saw her look out at us from the bright white square of light over the sink, I beckoned to her with one hand. Here! I was telling her. Come out here! But all she did was wave back at me cheerfully. So there was nothing left to do but go inside.

"No stew!" warned Chrissy by way of greeting Marsha.

She stared at him, uncomprehending. "What?"

"He thinks we're having stew. I told him that to keep him outside. Where's Dad?" I peered around the living room while hanging up my own jacket, then the smaller one with furry lining I'd pulled off Chrissy.

Dad's recliner was empty; he wasn't in the kitchen.

Marsha was setting the table and pouring milk. She gave a small laugh. "Why would you want to keep your brother outside? It's freezing."

I shrugged, not wanting to explain. I'd made up my mind to do what I'd been thinking about the whole time we were on the swing. "Where is he?" I started up the stairs. A moment later I was coming down again. "Where did Dad go? He's not in his room."

Marsha turned to face me, a glass in one hand, carton of milk in the other. "You'll have to wait to talk with him, Josie. He's gone for a walk."

"Then I'll catch up with him." I ran for the door.

Halfway across the living room, her hand seized my sleeve. "Don't, Josie. Don't go out there." Her green eyes flickered uncertainly, and the trembling in her fingertips passed through the sleeve of my sweatshirt, making the skin on my arm rise in goose bumps.

"I have to talk to him about Vietnam," I told her,

pulling away. "I have to let him know I want to help him. I want to hear what happened to him."

"Josie." She sighed deeply, shaking her head. "Leave him alone."

I stared at her for a minute, then stepped away. "No. No, I won't leave him alone. He needs someone to talk to. Has he told you about the war? Has he told you why he's so scared?"

"No." She looked away and I guessed she was hurt that he hadn't confided in her. She snapped around again. "Josie," she said urgently, sensing I was about to move again, "there's something you should know. He's been having nightmares, waking up horribly disturbed in the middle of the night."

"Since when?" I asked scowling at her.

"Oh, a long time, a couple years. But," she added hastily, "it's only been in the past month — with all this publicity about some vets returning to Vietnam — that things have . . . become so difficult for him." She gave me a wan smile and stepped closer. "We have to give him our support and let him work this out as best he — "

"He hurt Chrissy today," I broke in.

She froze, and a look of disbelief slid over her eyes. "No. He wouldn't — "

"He did," I insisted. "He spaced out completely and started blubbering about needing to protect Chrissy from someone. Then he grabbed Chrissy and squeezed him so hard Chrissy started to cry. I had to take him away from Dad, out of the house."

Marsha stood absolutely still, then glanced at Chrissy, who was emptying a box of puzzle pieces into the middle of the floor. He looked in marvelous shape.

"All right," I tossed over my shoulder, flinging wide the door, "don't believe me!"

Desperate to reach Dad before he got too far, I dashed across the front lawn where the strip of light from the gas lantern threw a pale shadow.

"Please, Josie!" Marsha was running to catch up.

Feeling angry with her, I stopped but wouldn't face her. I crossed my arms over my chest.

"Josie, don't go to him," she pleaded. "He's not . . . right. Listen, listen, hon . . ." She was breathing very hard, tears brimming in her pretty eyes as she stepped in front of me. "Come back inside. I have a surprise for you. You didn't give me a chance to tell you."

She tried on a smile and brushed one hand shakily across her cheek, wiping the wetness away with her fingertips.

Distrusting her, I simply glared through the spot where she stood.

She continued breathlessly. "I talked with my sister, Gloria, in Philadelphia today. She and Max would very much like us to drive down for Thanksgiving. I thought if we went a few days early, well, we'd have time for a nice long visit."

"You're doing it again," I said dully.

Marsha looked confused. "What?"

"You're hiding from everything. Is Dad coming?"

"Well," she murmured, gazing around us into the shadows, "if he could get away from work, for a day or two maybe . . ."

I threw up my hands. I don't believe this! I thought. "What work?" I shouted. "He's sold one damn house in over a month. Longer, for all I know. For all anyone tells me! You just want to take us away from him. Who's going to take care of my father? Who's going to take care of Jack Monroe?"

"Josie," she began with a sob, "I can't take responsibility for you or your brother's safety as long as we stay in this house, if what you're telling me about Chrissy is true. I didn't want to tell you this, but if it's the only way . . ." She looked at the ground near her feet. Her red hair frizzed around her flushed face, which was streaked and shining in the light of the street lamp. "Your father is so very frightened. And at night, he's especially in need of . . . reassurance. He's afraid of them coming back, I think, to kill him."

Them, who? I wondered. But only for an instant. I remembered what he'd said earlier about protecting Chrissy. I stared at Marsha's bowed head in horror. "You mean, the men he fought while he was in the army?" I gasped.

"The Viet Cong, the enemy." She nodded and clasped her hands in front of her. "Oh, Josie. One night he woke up and I don't believe he . . . recognized me." She lifted her eyes meaningfully to mine.

I thought about the anger and fear I'd caught in Dad's eyes more than once. And about the times he seemed to look straight through me, not only as if I weren't there but as if he were seeing someone other than me, his daughter.

"Did he hurt you?" I asked, my voice almost a whisper. Until that moment, I hadn't felt sorry for her at all. She'd just seemed to be making everything worse.

"Not really. Certainly not intentionally. And I never — I swear, I *never* thought he'd lay a hand on either you or Chrissy. But now" — her words dropped off — "I don't know. I just don't know." She bit her

134

lip as if debating her next words, holding them back another second or two. "Josie, at night he's been hiding something under his pillow. He wouldn't let me see it. But the other night I waited until he was asleep. Then I slipped my hand underneath. He has a knife. A kitchen knife hidden under his pillow."

I laughed nervously at her. I felt myself shaking my head, denying what she was trying to tell me. But all the while I knew it was true. If he was afraid of people coming to kill him, he'd find a way to protect himself, a weapon. Something he could carry around and no one would notice. I remembered the metallic glint in the chair cushion that night he'd been waiting up for me — or, at least, waiting for someone. And how he'd been disappearing for long stretches of time, mostly nights. Hiding from *them*? Or hunting them — trying to find the enemy before they found him.

I jammed my hands flat over my eyes and held on tight. This couldn't be happening to me, to us. It was crazy. A *knife*, for crying out loud?

"He loves us," I said out loud. "He loves us. He just hugged Chrissy a little too hard because he loves him so much."

"We don't know that," said Marsha, sounding miserable.

Again Dr. Whitehead's advice replayed in my mind. But how could I go to the police and complain about my own father?

Marsha burst into tears. "I tried to talk him into seeing a doctor, a counselor, anybody. That only made him worse; he just got angrier at me. Even the suggestion of seeing a professional makes him almost frantic. You saw him the other night, Josie!" So it wasn't her job he was steamed about. She'd told him he needed

135

a doctor. Maybe she'd gone so far as to call one, without asking him. "Damn it!" she cried when I said nothing. "I don't know what else to do."

Marsha never, ever swears. It was as much that as her actual words that shook me.

Behind my own ragged breathing and her sobs, I could hear Chrissy banging on something. Then he started to whine softly.

Marsha heard him, too, and swiveled toward the door. "We're going," she said, sounding determined. "I can't stay here with him, like this. I've been patient. I've tried to understand. Until now." She swiped at her eyes. "It's just too, too much."

"But, Marsha, he — "

"We're leaving tomorrow, straight after school." She started to run for the house as Chrissy's wails grew louder. "Get inside and pack a suitcase," she yelled over her shoulder.

I didn't move.

From the front lawn I watched the amber glow of the bay window. Inside, I could see Marsha lifting Chrissy off the top of the TV cabinet where he'd climbed and gotten stuck. She was patting him on the back, hugging him, kissing him on the ear to make him calm down. They looked like actors on a screen, with me out in the audience, not a part of them. Marsha and Chrissy, mother and son. I felt a tug at my heart. I should listen to her and go to them, and get hugged and told everything was going to be fine, just fine because we'd be going away.

But I looked down the road toward the woods where a dirt path disappeared into the night. It ran to the marsh and, eventually, to the beach. I couldn't leave my father out there, alone.

# CHAPTER NINETEEN

AFTER THE FIRST FEW FEET OF TREES THE PATH NARROWED to just wide enough for one person — hard-packed dirt, roots sticking up here and there. In the dark it would be easy to trip and fall. I had to stop running, and at that moment I noticed I was incredibly cold because in my rush to get out of the house I had left without my jacket. A flashlight would have helped, too.

A slim white crescent moon hung against the black space where the trees opened onto the marsh. I could smell the salt, heavy and sharp, and the air felt moister step by step.

At the woods' edge I paused and peered into the night. The tide was low. An endless stretch of cattails and shoulder-high blades of dune grass swayed in the wind. On the far side of the swamp was the shopping center, but all I could see was a red neon glow staining the horizon.

I turned south and started walking, keeping my right shoulder to the lights, left to the trees. I'd move as fast as I could for a quarter mile maybe, then try the other direction.

But I hadn't gone far before I saw him.

He was sitting on the ground with his back to a big, flat-topped boulder, his knees drawn up in front of him. He was watching those same red lights.

Afraid of startling him, I came up slowly.

"Dad," I called softly.

His face reflected the distant glow and wore absolutely no expression. I stepped closer and stooped about two feet away from him. His arms rested in a circle on the tips of his knees, and his hands were clasped. Between them a short, smooth blade caught the dull crimson neon.

For the longest time I couldn't take my eyes off that paring knife. I just knelt there, not daring to move. At last I noticed his lips begin to quiver rapidly, as if he were speaking to someone very close by.

"The tunnels," he murmured. "That's where they're coming from . . . got to go in . . . no choice this time. Fire fight, boys."

In the moonlight I could see the glint of his eyes sliding from side to side, restless, searching the distant treeline. Whenever the sea breeze eddied through a clump of tall grass, stirring it to rustling life, his gaze shifted that way.

I shivered again, watching the way his fingers curled and turned white around the handle of the knife. But I wasn't cold anymore. My palms were sweating something fierce. I rubbed the perspiration away on my jeans.

As he slowly rose, Dad held the blade out in front of him, the way men do in the movies if they're getting ready to fight. I'd never seen him hold a weapon except a trap gun. And that didn't seem to count.

"Mack," he called softly, still not aware I was there, "stay in close. Dorsey, Fox, Teague."

His men, I guessed. He's calling his men, getting them ready to move on. I wished I could see what he was seeing. Maybe the lights looked like flames to him. Maybe the marsh grass was something else — the enemy.

He continued to mutter. "Got to keep the perimeter clear."

His papers had said he was a platoon leader. He must

have had to take men out on raids, or whatever they were called.

"Damn tunnels, miles of them," he grunted feverishly. "Under the airstrips, for all we know. Got to clear them out. Get *them* before they get *us*."

He was moving forward with a purposeful stride, then circling in a crouch, mumbling now and then to his invisible men.

I sat on the soggy ground and stopped trying to understand the words. It's hopeless, I thought. And I started to cry silently.

More than anything, I wanted to cut out, and fast. This was what Marsha was running away from — these living nightmares — and I understood now why she felt she had to.

A very old woman used to live down the street from us. She must have been ninety, at least. She thought I was her kid sister; talking to her gave me the creeps. I guess people who are confused that way make anyone nervous. But this was ten times — a hundred times — worse.

I'd been with Dad all of my life. I'd been his responsibility alone after my mother left. Now someone had to take responsibility for him. If I turned my back on him when he was so helpless, I'd feel like a traitor.

Suddenly he shouted out, "Down! Hit dirt!" And he threw himself flat, the knife flying out of his hand.

Good, I thought. But I kept an eye on the cold glint in the grass.

He stayed so still, for so long, I didn't know what to do. At last I stood up, wiped away the tears with my shirt sleeve, and cautiously walked over to where he lay. Not until I was right next to him could I see that his eyes were wide open.

He blinked at my shoes, which were inches from his nose, then leaped to his feet.

Gasping in surprise, I pleaded, "Dad, it's me. Please let's go home. You're not in Vietnam! You're in Connecticut. Think!"

I couldn't be sure he heard me. He wore an astonished look on his face, so maybe he had.

Then he cocked his arms as if he were now holding some sort of gun. Not his trap gun — the stance was all wrong. His hands were lower, placed wider. And he deliberately, ever so slowly, rotated to face — me.

His index finger made a frantic pumping motion. Then his arms fell to his sides, letting the phantom gun drop. He looked around, a desolate expression in his gray eyes. And he called his men, one by one.

I stood very still, feeling the chill air hit my skin. My father, at least in his imagination, had just shot me!

But, as shocked and terrified as I was, I couldn't seem to move when he walked up even closer to me. Stretching out one hand, he skimmed it over my hair, the way he had tried to do in the living room while Mary was there. It was as if he were knocking off a hat or scarf to get a better look at my face.

He groaned, and sheer horror replaced the sorrowful expression in his eyes.

"Fox," he said, his voice trembling. "My God. A *gai que* . . . just a girl! What the hell's she doing out here after dark?"

One rough palm touched either side of my face. "Dad," I whispered between them, "please come home with me. You're not at Tan Son Nhut anymore. Come with me, it's Josie."

He evidently didn't hear me. "Can't be more than

140

thirteen, fourteen tops," he moaned, throwing his head back. Then he glared at me, furious again. "What on God's green earth were you *doing* out here?" he shrieked. "The villagers have been warned; anything moves out here after sundown is fair game! You know that, damn you!"

Releasing me, he spun away, shoulders slumped, tears flowing down his cheeks. "I killed her. A kid. Oh, Lord! Fox," he groaned hollowly. "Teague, Dorsey, Smith — where *are* you?"

He seemed to have worn himself down. I stepped up beside him without saying a word. Immediately he leaned heavily on my shoulder and started walking.

I can't say he realized I was there at first. I steered him away from the marsh, down the path toward home. But somewhere before we reached Tyler Road, I knew the flashback was over because he said my name.

## CHAPTER TWENTY

"T.G.I.F!" SHOUTED MARTY FORD AS WE STEPPED OFF the bus in front of school.

Mary Chang granted him a weak smile but walked straight past him and through the main entrance.

Baffled, I stared after her, then ran to catch up. "Did I miss something?" The shadow of last night still hung over me. I'd been so preoccupied on the bus I'd hardly spoken to Mary.

She shrugged. But when we reached the lockers, she waited in silence while I hung up my jacket.

"Marty and I broke up last night," she said at last, her voice just a little nasal, as if she were coming down with a cold. "It's no big deal."

I checked out her eyes, but she wasn't even close to crying. "Whose idea was that?" I asked. "Because if it's his, he's a bigger jerk than I thought. You're better than he deserves."

"Mine," she said tersely. "I didn't actually tell him we were through. He understands though."

"Oh?" Martin Ford had never seemed especially perceptive of anything, let alone another person's feelings.

She blew a puff of air at her shiny ebony bangs and they fluttered across her forehead. "We went out last night."

"You and the goon squad?"

She laughed a little, tightly. "Just Marty and me and another couple. Anyway, it was all right when I went with the guys before. I mean, they're all regular guys. I felt special, you see, because they took me along with them."

"Give me a break." I pulled out two books I'd need for first class.

"No, really, Josie. Boys just *never* pay attention to me. You know that."

"That's not true. You always shake them off whenever they try to get near you." I saw the look of despair cross her eyes, the one she got when she was disappointed with herself. "But that's all right," I assured her quickly. "Being shy, or waiting for the right guy. That's cool. That's smart."

"Oh, smart. Yeah." I was just trying to cheer her up. But she looked worse now and shook her head. A tear glimmered at the corner of one eye. "Josie. Honestly, it's not just because of Marty I'm upset. I have to tell you something totally off the floor."

"Off the wall," I corrected automatically.

It was close to last bell. I was no longer paying very close attention to Mary because I was thinking about all the work I had to hand in, or pick up by the end of the day. I couldn't afford to start late.

I hadn't seen Marsha before I left for school. But last night I'd told her about Dad's flashback, and she'd been so upset I was sure she'd have the car packed by the time I got home.

Why did Mary Chang pick today to be on the verge of a crying jag? "Tell me what Marty did," I insisted while keeping her moving toward her own locker.

She sighed. "That has nothing to do with — "

"Tell me," I demanded impatiently.

She winced. "Well, okay. The other times all we did was ride around town for an hour or so, talking about the games and who was playing what position. And sometimes I even made suggestions when the other guys asked for ideas about where to take their dates to dinner before homecoming dance. Honestly, Josie, it was nothing bad, nothing at all."

"But this time?"

"Fran Jeffers came with us last night." She let the words out in one breath.

So, there it was. I had a fair picture of what the night had been like.

"Was she high?" I asked.

"I think so, but not much. She laughed a lot. I don't know. Maybe she was, more than I thought." She leaned back against the locker door so I couldn't open it. "That isn't the point. What I have to tell you is about my parents."

I glanced down the length of the hall and saw Perry disappearing into his classroom. I had some of the back work I owed him; I'd hoped to get to homeroom early and finish another assignment for him. Timing didn't look good now.

"Did they tell you to break up with Marty?" I tried to hurry the conversation along.

"Will you quit with Marty?" She stomped her foot, startling me because she was never this angry. Her eyes were button black and shining and urgent. "All right. If you *have* to know, Jerry, the other guy, screwed Fran in the backseat. Marty wanted me to do it, too. When I wouldn't, he got in back with Fran. *That's* why I broke up with Marty."

She was really crying now, swallowing big sobs.

Maybe if my own life hadn't been so insane I would have been kinder to her. I'm usually a very good friend. I like to help people with their problems, but before this I'd never had trouble coping with life myself. How do I bring up my C in Biology II? What color lipstick won't make me look like a hooker? That sort of thing I could handle! Even the stuff Marty had pulled was manageable. But living with a crazy soldier and an invisible army . . .

I couldn't take any more. "You're so damn naive!" I blurted out above the noise of classroom doors slamming. "I can't believe you didn't see that coming."

She looked so pitiful standing there, avoiding my furious glare. At last I put an arm around her shoulders and squeezed her.

"I could take a machete to Martin Ford right here and now," I said loyally. How could he do something so horrible to such a nice girl as Mary?

She was shaking her head. "It wasn't so bad, it really wasn't. I just got out of the car and started walking. I was too mad at Marty and too angry with myself for

144

not seeing what a shallow person he really was to feel sorry I'd lost him. And honestly, Josie, I'm glad I know. But what I had to tell you — and I didn't want to have to — is that we're moving."

My mouth dropped open in shock. "You're what?"

She nodded sadly. "Probably before the beginning of next semester. My father put money down on a house in Ledyard, where my uncle lives."

"I — I don't understand." My best friend would be a long distance call away and going to a different school. Why? "That's a lot longer commute to your father's work," I said vaguely.

The last bell rang. Neither of us moved. Only a few people flashed by, late slips in hand.

"He feels safer there." Mary gnawed her lower lip. "That's not quite true. I will feel safer there, too, Josie. Your father scares us. My dad thought he saw someone peering in a window at us one night, several weeks ago. It happened a few more times, and he called the police. They didn't do anything except check our locks. When my father heard about how your dad freaked out when he saw me the other day — "

"You *told* him?" I cried.

Mary backed off a step. "I was scared. I had to, Josie." Tears welled in her eyes. "What was I supposed to do? Wait for him to jump me some night? I was terrified walking home alone in the dark last night. And it wasn't because of Marty. I can handle him. I kept thinking your father might mistake me for some villager in Vietnam and attack me. *Josie, I've never even been in Vietnam!*"

Neither had I, but I still felt as if I were taking part in a war: Dad's war that had never ended. I hugged her and told her I was sorry her family was going to have to move because of us. I didn't tell her about Marsha's evacuation plans.

I worked straight through lunch, used study hall and every other free minute to try to catch up on assignments. If Marsha was going to drag me off to her sister's house, I wasn't going to leave all that work undone.

At the end of the day I turned in everything I had done and picked up assignments through Thanksgiving vacation. All the teachers wished me a pleasant trip.

When I got home I expected to find Marsha slinging suitcases into the car. Instead, she was in her leotard, doing a workout she'd taped on the VCR.

"I've decided to take this one day at a time," she puffed between jumping jacks.

I knew she wasn't talking about exercise. "You mean, we're not going to Philly?"

"We'll see" was all she'd say, but she was smiling dimly as the music picked up pace. Her thighs were tight and hard where the leotard cut high, nearly to her hip bones. I thought she looked really sexy. I wished my legs were that long.

She talked in spurts between jumps. "Your father slept well last night — straight through without waking even once. That's the first time in months." She flashed me a grin. "I think it's a good sign."

I watched her warily. The floor sagged slightly each time she landed. "Did he put another knife under his pillow?" I asked cynically.

"No," she said, and stopped bouncing even though the three women demonstrating weren't done. She walked over to me and rested her hands on my shoulders. A fine trail of sweat beaded her brow and disappeared into the terry strip across her forehead. "You were right, Josie. He needed to talk out his feelings, his memories. I hadn't been able to help him do that."

"Are you saying you think he's better?" I asked.

"Definitely. He was exhausted when you two came home last night, but he seemed much calmer as well. I honestly believe he's going to be all right now. You just keep on talking to him."

I wasn't so sure. "Do you think he'd see a professional counselor?" I asked.

She thought for a moment. "I don't know about that right now. But perhaps before too long he'd agree."

I decided I should telephone Dr. Whitehead and ask him.

I walked to Mary's house and asked if I could use the telephone in her room. She sat on the bed while I dialed and looked surprised when she saw it was a long distance number.

"I'm having it charged to our phone," I told her.

She looked embarrassed. "It's okay," she said. "You don't have to."

This time Whitehead came straight on the line. I told him about the flashback and he was very quiet until I'd finished. "He definitely needs professional help, Josephine. Hearing him use my name startled me until I remembered our code. "Has he actually hurt anyone during these episodes?"

I hesitated. "No," I told him at last.

He could hear the indecision in my voice. "But you're scared, more than before."

"Only of not doing the right thing," I said. "What if I'm making him worse? What if interrupting his flashback was the wrong thing to do?"

"No," he assured me. "You did just right, Josephine. Your father is dealing with a lot of guilt and something called a post-traumatic stress disorder. PTSD. His mind alternates between dealing with reality and replaying the scenes that most disturb him from when he was in Vietnam. If you hadn't interrupted his flashback, he might have continued living it for many hours, possibly for days. Your interruption caused what's called a startle response — which is good. You startled him out of it. You reminded him of today, reality."

He was silent for a while, then continued very seriously in a low, calm voice. "He won't come to see me, Josephine?"

"I can try. But I don't think so."

"Try," he said. "Try very hard. And don't wait too long."

# CHAPTER TWENTY-ONE

THAT NIGHT DAD CONTINUED TO BE OKAY, EVEN TO BE functioning in ways he hadn't for a long time. His gray eyes seemed clear and less terror stricken. And he didn't disappear on one of his reconnaissance missions.

Saturday, Marsha declared that the Philly trip was postponed indefinitely; she called Gloria. "Maybe for Christmas," she told her sister in a consoling voice. I could tell she was secretly thrilled that we were staying. And I felt a lot better to know Dad wouldn't be left alone.

Sunday morning at nine Dad strode across the kitchen, beaming at all of us. "Anyone for Dunkin' Donuts?" he asked.

Marsha smiled happily. She was scheduled to go in to work at noon — just for a couple hours to relieve other cashiers during their lunch break. Turning to Chrissy, she asked, "How about a second breakfast, big boy? Would you like a doughnut?"

We used to go for coffee and doughnuts every Sunday morning. I love the crusty, old-fashioned, sour cream ones, sprinkled with confectioner's sugar. I learned to drink coffee just so I could dunk them.

But that day I had other things on my mind. I hadn't had a chance to talk to Brian for days.

Dad turned to me and raised one brow in question. "Don't feel like it this morning," I apologized. "Got to start watching my waistline." I patted my stomach under the jeans, hoping there was enough bulge to make my excuse sound believable. "Put on a few pounds lately."

"Well," said Dad, looking only a little disappointed, "if you're sure."

As soon as they'd pulled out of the drive, I headed for the phone.

"I don't like you being there with him," Brian said when I'd filled him in on what had been happening. "Maybe Marsha's idea to get you and Chrissy away from him wasn't so bad."

"Brian! You *want* me to go to Philadelphia? We'd be hundreds of miles apart. You and me."

He was quiet.

"It's better this way," I told him firmly. "If he'll talk this out, even a little at a time, maybe soon I can convince him to go see Dr. Whitehead."

"Maybe." He sounded as if he was talking into his collar, all muffled, the way he does when he's nervous.

"Look, I'd like to come over and be there next time you speak with him about the war."

"No," I said quickly.

"Why not?" He was irritated now. "So what if he hates my guts? I can talk to him, reassure him. I'm a great listener; you have to be in a big family."

"Bri," I reminded him, "he's got some sort of irrational negative set against you. I don't think he'll want to open up with you there. Don't take it personally," I added.

He thought for a while, then let go of a long breath. "I suppose you're right. But I want to see you."

I smiled into the phone. His needing me as much as I needed him gave me a warm tingle. Again, I thought about how our love was the only security I had these days. I closed my eyes and sighed, as much from happiness that he cared as from frustration that my parents wanted us apart. "I'm watching Chrissy until Marsha gets home, then I work tonight," I said.

"Good. I'll get the car and meet you at Harvey's before closing."

But later that afternoon Marsha called from the store. "I'll have to stay longer than I'd expected," she explained. "One of the cashiers can't make it in because her daughter just came down with the chicken pox. How will you ever get to work?"

"I'll get a ride with Mary," I suggested.

She didn't respond.

"Isn't that all right?"

"Oh, yes," she said softly. Then I knew she was worried about something else. "That's just fine, Josie. I was only thinking what to do about Chrissy."

"I'll take Chrissy over to Mrs. Bedloe when I'm ready to leave," I said quickly, although Dad was upstairs, working on some new listings for houses.

"I think that's best," she agreed.

CHRISSY WAS NAPPING, SO I MADE AN EARLY SUPPER OF soup and grilled cheese sandwiches for myself. After I'd eaten I put a second serving on a tray and took it upstairs. Dad's door was closed. I knocked.

"Yo!" he called out.

Happy to hear his voice sounding more normal each time we talked, I walked in. He was sprawled on the bed in the middle of a nest of paperwork. I thought how much we were alike. This must be how I look when I have all my homework out.

"Figured you might be hungry," I said. "You haven't had anything since this morning."

"Must have eaten a half-dozen doughnuts though." He grinned, setting aside the yellow legal pad and the pen he'd been writing with. "That can carry you awhile."

I laughed.

"What kind of soup?" he asked, eyeing the steaming bowl and sitting up. He looked slim and his skin seemed on the gray side. I guessed he hadn't caught up on his sleep or his appetite. During the summer he'd gone to the beach every day, taking a long midafternoon lunch since he often worked nights. He was one of the few people you ever saw actually swimming laps between the beach and the raft about three hundred yards offshore. Now, his tan was fading and the muscles in his upper arms looked soft. He was still handsome though, I thought proudly.

"Minestrone," I announced, placing the tray across his lap, "and grilled cheese, double cheese."

"Just the way I like it." He grinned.

151

I kissed him on the bridge of his nose, like always, and sat on the bed watching him eat. At last I couldn't wait any longer.

"Do you remember Thursday night?" I asked, holding my breath. Neither of us had spoken about it.

He lifted the spoon to his mouth and sipped, his eyes focusing on the bowl. "I remember, Josephine." He put down his spoon and reached over to pull my head down and kiss it on top, the way he did to Chrissy. "Nights, they get bad for me sometimes."

I nodded, watching his eyes, wondering what else he'd seen that I didn't know about — and he wished he never had. "You thought you were in Vietnam, at Tan Son Nhut."

His face turned a shade paler. The faint stubble of tan beard looked almost black against his cheeks. "I'm sorry," he said ashamedly. "I wish to God, Josie, you hadn't seen me."

"It's all right." I leaned my head on his chest. "I think it must have been horrible there."

"Yeah," my father murmured, "it was that." He moved the tray aside onto the bedspread and hugged me. I sensed he needed to be held even more than I did. "I have to leave the house sometimes," he whispered into my hair. "I just think it's best. You've seen what happens when I don't, how I tear Marsha apart. None of this is her fault. I'm to blame." I felt his jaw clench near my brow. "What I did has come back to me, and — " he stopped abruptly.

"What you did?"

He was silent.

I pushed away from him. "Dad, what happened to you at Tan Son Nhut?"

He shook his head, watching his hands folded over his lap.

"Dad?"

"A lot. Too much. If I ever told you, you'd hate me, Josie."

His voice quavered and sent chills up my spine. Without intending to, I gripped the side of the bed for support. "I'll never hate you," I told him.

His eyes lifted to meet mine. Then he began. "As we left the compound, we were always so wired — aware of everything around us. Snipers could be hiding behind a grass screen ahead, booby traps buried in the rice paddies . . ." He paused and a queer expression slipped into his eyes, then faded. "Just so many things could kill you in a matter of seconds. So, if something moved out there, you fired first, looked later. There was a girl. She must have heard us coming and been terrified. She must have hidden in the brush near one of the Viet Cong tunnel entrances. But I saw the branches move . . . and I . . . shot her."

"Oh," I said, my throat and eyes burning.

"I don't understand what's happening to me," he continued. "I thought I was dealing with it all right. Then one day I took out my trap gun and I couldn't stand to hold it anymore. I sold it. I wanted to sell yours, too."

"I know."

"I can't figure why, but it all started coming back to me. I saw you with the kerchief over your head — and I swear to God, you were *her*. Then your friend Mary . . ." His words faded away.

"She reminds you of the people over there," I said.

"Yes."

I shut my eyes hard enough to see white sparks exploding against my lids. What would it be like to know you'd killed a person who'd innocently gotten mixed up in a war, who didn't even want to be a part of it? To kill a girl just my age?

"But you can't keep running away from what happened," I said quietly. "There are people who can help you — help us, Dad." I held my breath. "There's a place in New Haven where a lot of veterans go for help. I have the phone number."

"And then we can all sit around and tell tales about the friends we saw blown to pieces?" He moved me aside so he could stretch out his legs. I didn't want to look at his face because I could hear the pain in his voice. "No," he said flatly, "that's not for me. Dredging up more of the past, then having to live with it all over again — uh-uh. That's done with. No shrink is going to change what was, or make it go away. No one can bring back those men, the children. . . ."

I sat very quietly on the edge of his bed, not saying anything.

He breathed raggedly for several seconds, then swallowed. As his eyes filled up, he looked toward the window. "It's going to be okay, Josie. We'll make it."

"Sure," I said, picking up the tray and turning quickly away. I didn't want Dad to see the doubt in my face.

AT FIVE I GOT CHRISSY READY TO GO TO THE SITTER'S. I wasn't as positive, now, that I was doing Dad any good. Maybe facing the past was something he really couldn't handle. Maybe by shoving it at him, I was making it all worse. I decided to ask Brian to check at the library to see if Dr. Whitehead's package had come. Maybe

154

something he'd sent would help me decide what to do next.

Mrs. Bedloe opened the door onto her porch and smiled stoically down at Chrissy, who was tugging at my hand, trying to escape and run home again. She seized him under the arms, lifting him to her hip. Mrs. Bedloe is fat and he has to spread his legs twice as wide to straddle her as he does with Marsha. He wriggled and made a nasty face at me for turning traitor.

"I was surprised when your mother called to ask me to watch Chrissy today," Mrs. Bedloe said, and it occurred to me that she probably had other things planned for the day and wasn't too thrilled to have to baby-sit after doing it all week. "I'd expected your father would be available to take care of your brother. Isn't Jack home?" She peered around the end of the porch. Dad's car was clearly visible in the drive.

I shifted my feet and elaborated on Marsha's excuse. "He has to show a house in Mystic later today."

How could I tell her that Marsha didn't trust him to take care of his own kid? And that I agreed with her?

## CHAPTER TWENTY-TWO

ON THE WAY TO HARVEY'S, MARY CHANG SNIFFLED constantly. "A cold," she explained. "I get rid of one pain in the neck, and now this."

"You do look awful," I told her later that night. Her eyes were pink and watery. She blew her nose into a lace-trimmed handkerchief. "Why don't you go home?" I suggested. "I'll cover your booths."

Loading a tray with platters of burgers and fries she

said weakly, "I drove tonight, remember? How would you get home?"

I followed her to the counter where she served Ted Murskey, one of her regulars. He grinned at her, his freckles practically popping out of his face. Mary hardly blinked at him before moving on to the next customer. She must have been totally out of it to have missed his enraptured expression.

"Brian's coming by later," I said.

She gave me a strange look.

"Hey," I demanded, "you aren't on my parents' side, are you?"

"I just don't want to see you get in any more trouble with your father," she said quickly, blowing her nose again.

I studied her expression. She was honestly worried about me. "All right. I'll call Marsha and ask if it's all right, this once, for him to drive me home. She'll be so exhausted from working overtime she won't want to come get me anyway."

When Brian arrived at Harvey's at nine, he was wearing his pale blue lambswool sweater and tan cords. The blue made his eyes look lighter. His dark hair spun in soft corkscrews down the back of his neck. He smiled at me and my heart double timed a few beats before I turned back to the order I was taking. For the next hour he sat alone in the back booth. I brought him a plate of onion rings and a Coke. He studied from a history text and took notes while eating his onions.

At closing we walked out together, his arm around my waist.

I leaned my head against his shoulder, feeling tired and vaguely worried. "I called Marsha a couple times — to let her know you'd be bringing me home.

Got nothing but a busy signal. Maybe somebody left the phone off the hook." I sighed. "I suppose you'd better leave me at the end of Tyler, or else in front of Mary's house."

"This is crazy, Josie," Brian said sadly. He unwrapped his arm to stick the key in the car door. I slid under the steering wheel, then over to the middle of the seat. He got in next to me and started the car.

There was a small, brown, padded mailer on the seat. "That's the stuff you asked me to pick up from the library," he told me. The postmark was New Haven.

"Thanks," I said. "I'll read it tonight."

It took three or four minutes for the defroster to clear the windshield. I wedged my fingers between my knees to warm them. When Brian saw me, he turned up the heater.

"Did you talk to him?" he asked in a low voice as we drove through the dark glades south of the airport. Long lines of blue landing lights glowed from the left side of the road. A Pilgrim commuter circled down toward the field, the tiny lights on its underside blinking. You could hear the jets straining to cut back.

I nodded sadly, about to tell him how looking at me every day had hurt my father, and how thinking of Brian with a gun probably brought back the memory of the Vietnamese boys and possibly even some of his own men who hadn't survived to come home. But I stopped myself. Brian was already worried enough.

"I was thinking," he began, "it must be hard on your dad, you and Marsha both working. He must feel really rotten, not being able to feed his own family. That would drive my old man nuts."

"Working," I murmured. Then I laughed out loud. "What's so funny?"

I shook my head. "More like strange," I said quietly, "not really funny. I took a job just to get pocket change, just money for messing around with, you know. For pizza and movies and clothes. But now I don't think we Monroes can do without it."

I slipped my fingers into my jacket pocket and stroked the roughly mended seam. Coins wear through cloth, I thought. Their thin edges rub and rub until they work their way through — like memories temporarily tucked away in the mind. They eventually fall out . . . and there they are. A Vietnamese girl dead with my father standing over her, crying.

Brian turned the corner into Tyler. I was watching the yellow patch of pavement under our headlights. I felt him straighten on the seat next to me. And he readjusted his grip on the steering wheel.

"Josie," he whispered, "something's . . ."

I looked up slowly and saw a swarm of red and blue lights farther down the road. From a distance it looked like a street carnival.

Brian slowed the Pinto as we got closer. People were standing outside on their lawns. Mrs. Bedloe in her flowered muu-muu. Her husband next to her. The Aronsons, our next-door neighbors, had joined them. A gang of neighborhood boys were running up and down the street, shouting excitedly, until a lady yelled at them to go home and they took off. An ambulance and at least three police cars blocked the road, their lights flashing.

Brian stopped the car before we got too close and turned on the seat to face me.

My eyes felt hot and so dry it hurt to blink. "Oh, Bri." I choked. "What has he done?"

# CHAPTER TWENTY-THREE

ONE CRUISER BLOCKED THE MIDDLE OF THE STREET. THE colored bar on its hood zipped back and forth, throwing flashes into the night against the maple trees and gray shingles of the houses.

I threw open the Pinto's door and ran, panting and tasting the salt in the cold wind every time I gasped for breath, never seeming to get enough air.

"Josie, stop!" Brian's voice seemed distant, but I could hear his sneakers slapping the cold pavement behind me.

Ahead of us an amplified voice kept saying something over and over, probably something calming like, "There's nothing to be afraid of." Except the bullhorn confused the words so it sounded like an unintelligible growl that ended in a vicious taunt: "afraid of . . . afraid of . . . afraid. . . ."

Brian tackled me around the waist and held on to keep me from falling. He shouted close to my ear, "They won't let you get anywhere near, Josie!"

I swallowed hot tears and slashed at his arms. "Let me go! I have to find out what's happened."

I could count all of the cruisers now. One at either end of the block, two more pulled up nose to nose on the Murphy's lawn directly across the street from our house — four altogether. The ambulance was farther down.

Dark figures crouched behind each car. A bright beam of light had been aimed at our bay window so that it looked the way it might at Christmas if we'd spotlighted the front of the house. Only that night our house looked little and meek, as though it were cringing and trying to slip away from the harsh green beam.

"I have to see," I insisted but gave up struggling. I went limp and leaned against Brian's chest.

For a minute he said nothing, then he just took my hand and started walking purposefully toward the nearest cruiser.

The street was quiet, except for the bullhorn. As we got closer I could make out more people standing in the long blue shadows of their houses or watching silently out their windows. I began to shake.

"What has he done?" I didn't know I'd actually said it out loud until Brian answered.

"We'll see. Just stay cool. It may look worse than it really — Hey! There's Marsha."

She was sitting in the backseat of the first cruiser. The door was open, and a man in a baggy white cotton suit was stooping beside her. He was looking up into her face and talking while he put a syringe away into a small metal suitcase. Marsha's head hung down in her hands, and I couldn't see her eyes.

She glanced up when I said her name. Her face was white — absolutely chalk-white inside the frame of her red hair. Her eyes were unfocused. She pressed her lips along a thin purple line.

"You'd better go back home," said the guy in white who looked too young to be a doctor.

A cop appeared and stood nearby, listening.

"This *is* my home," I said, unable to take my eyes off Marsha.

The cop was suddenly alert. "Get in the car," he ordered me in a grim voice.

I stared up at him. "What happened? What's going on?" I demanded, without budging.

He plunked a hand on my shoulder, but I pulled out from under it. Then a guarded expression fell over his eyes, under the stiff brim of his cap. We stood, watching each other, for another minute. I didn't like the way he was ordering me around without telling me why or what was going on. And I suppose he was surprised I hadn't just done what he'd said, simply because he was a cop.

The sound of shattering glass broke through the night. "Down!" exploded a command from somewhere. Immediately the ambulance attendant squatted and pushed Marsha's head down. The cop dragged Brian and me onto the pavement with him.

The loud report of a gun boomed through the air, followed by a shout. "Get away from my house! You, get the hell away! Leave me alone!"

"He's shooting at them!" I glanced at Brian. He shook his head, his way of saying: Sorry, Josie, it's all over. Nothing we can do anymore.

I closed my eyes. My head was pounding. Why couldn't I think straight? There had to be something. . . .

Still squatting like a baseball catcher, the cop yanked a walkie-talkie out of a leather hip holster and started talking into it very fast.

"He has my gun," I whispered to Brian.

He winced but said, "Yeah. I figured."

"Your mother will be all right," said the attendant. "I gave her something to calm her down."

That was just too much. I glared at him. "She's been calm for weeks," I snapped. "She doesn't need shots!"

But I knew it was too late. What did it matter if she floated?

The night air felt suddenly colder. I touched my face and was surprised to find it wet. All around us cops and strangers ducked and ran and slunk through shadows. I thought about Dad alone in our house. If he was in the middle of a flashback he must be terrified — all these people surrounding him, flashing lights, waving guns.

"Move it back!" croaked a voice over the walkie-talkie. "We're getting a sharpshooter from the state police."

I spun and glared at the cop who held the radio. He spoke into it. "What's Monroe's range?"

"*I* don't know, Verbine! Just get the hell back before one of these — "

Another crack sent the shadowy line of uniforms down again.

I drew a deep breath and said, "A Browning Citori twenty-eight-gauge over-under is accurate up to about one hundred yards."

The send switch must have been pushed down. "Who's the ballistics expert?" demanded the walkie-talkie.

Verbine gave me an odd look. "Monroe's daughter. She says it's her gun." So, he'd been listening in while Brian and I talked.

Then my eyes dropped to the walkie-talkie in his hand. And I edged forward.

"A hundred yards, she says. Sounds like a sporting shotgun, for duck or — "

I lunged for the black box. Yanking it out of the cop's hands, I yelled into it, "I want to go inside and see

162

him! He's my father. He'll talk to me!"

"Verbine" — the disembodied voice sounded aggravated — "get her out of there."

"It's my fault!" I cried. "It's my gun!" And I'm one reason he can't forget about Vietnam, I added silently.

The cop wrestled the speaker out of my hand and flicked it off.

"Look," he said, trying to be patient. "We've done this sort of thing before, so we know how to handle your father. All we want is for him to throw out his gun. Then we'll get him to a hospital. Okay? Nobody's going to shoot at him, so long as he doesn't hurt anyone or try to leave here with that gun. Now," he said in an official tone, "get in the cruiser."

But I didn't. First of all, I didn't believe the Groton Police Department had *any* experience disarming Nam vets. I would have read about it in the paper. Second, I *knew* Dad couldn't walk out of our house as long as a couple dozen armed men were pointing guns at him.

"My father's just scared," I explained to the sergeant. "You can tell he's aiming over our heads. He'll stop and calm down if you leave. Let me go in to him."

The ambulance attendant shook his head sympathetically at the cop. "That's all you need. Right, Sarge? Another one in there."

The hairs on the back of my neck stood up. Standing rigid, I glared at the attendant, then Verbine. "What does he mean, 'another one'?" I demanded.

"Nothing, sis." The cop's and attendant's eyes met meaningfully. "Just get in the car. We're moving back so you won't get hurt."

Without further explanation, he clamped one hand on my head and pressed down hard. Losing my balance,

I toppled into the backseat next to Marsha.

"You, too, son," Sergeant Verbine said, and opened the front passenger door for Brian.

Immediately I looked around the inside of the cruiser. No handles on the inside for the backseat. But neither door was closed all the way. I glanced back over my shoulder. Verbine stood in front of one rear door, his body blocking it. But his attention was on Brian, who was arguing with him. Marsha slumped against the seat, her eyes closed.

"Where's Chrissy?" I whispered, still not wanting to believe what the attendant had let slip — my little brother was inside the house with Dad. I could guess what had happened. Eager to have time to herself, Mrs. Bedloe had noticed that Dad's car hadn't moved from the driveway and brought Chrissy home. But I had to be sure.

"*Where is Chrissy?*" I repeated, shaking Marsha by the shoulders.

Her green eyes bloodshot from crying, she peered at me from beneath heavy lids. My anger melted away. I took her hand between mine; it was freezing. When I squeezed it, tears oozed between her lashes and her lips trembled.

"Oh, no." I groaned.

At last the sergeant made Brian climb into the front seat, then slammed the door after him.

"I'm sorry, Josie," Brian muttered without turning around. "I tried to convince him. You know," he began in his mature, consoling tone, "you're probably safer here. Your dad just doesn't understand what he's doing. He might not even recognize you, and there's no telling what . . ."

I watched Verbine through the side window. When

164

he turned to say something to the ambulance driver, I crawled over Marsha's legs, along the seat, and flung open the other door. Then I ran across the street and through the nearest yard straight toward my house.

# CHAPTER TWENTY-FOUR

THE HEDGE OF MOUNTAIN LAUREL THAT RUNS ALONG THE west end of our house is almost six feet high. Chrissy and I play Tiger-and-Hunter in it. He gets scared if I'm the Tiger, so I'm always the Hunter. And he always eats me.

I zigzagged across our neighbors' lawns, jumped Marsha's dead tomato vines, and raced straight for the good old laurel. Once I got there — if I got there — no one would be able to spot me. They'd have to come right in after me.

A whoop of surprise and alarm went up from behind the line of police cars. Verbine, I supposed, must have blown the whistle. Suddenly the piercing green lights flashed off, and I couldn't see where I was going. But neither could Dad see me running across the front lawn.

I wasn't managing to stoop and run very well at the same time, so I hoped my father didn't choose that moment to start firing blindly.

"Hey, hold up there!" a man shouted.

Out of the corner of one eye I caught a dim flash. Steps pounded behind me. But I didn't answer him and I didn't slow down.

Then the shooting began again.

Flinging myself down on the dark grass, I clutched the blades in my fists, breathing huge heaving wheezes into them. Twisting around, I tried to see who'd been following.

A young cop in dark blue was spread-eagled face forward on the ground. He was only ten feet behind me, and he looked up so that our eyes met. Without a word, he started inching on hands and knees toward me.

"Go back!" I hissed. "He won't hurt me. I need to talk to him."

"Kid," he grunted, still crawling, "he's not in the mood for conversation. We put your mother on the telephone from a neighbor's house. Didn't do any good. Your old man cut the line."

"He'll listen to me," I insisted.

The cop inched closer. "Come back with me before we both get shot."

I started to move away from him, but as soon as he saw I wasn't giving in he lunged out from his knees and got hold of one of my shoes.

I kicked at his fingers with my free foot. After what seemed forever, the white leather slipped from his grip. Jumping up, I sprinted full out for the hedge.

Behind me, I heard him scuffle to his feet. Almost immediately gunfire opened up again and my heart stopped dead in my chest, although my legs kept working.

I ducked under branches.

"You stupid man!" I panted, crouching behind the leafy screen. Not the cop — Dad. What if he actually hit someone? Acting nutso and holing up in your own house was one thing. Gunning people down on your front lawn, though, wasn't going to be easy to explain. And then there was my secret fear, the one that first hit me the night Chrissy and I spent on the swing . . .

166

No. I wouldn't think about that now.

I shrank deeper into the shrubs, gasping so hard my sides ached. My eyes burned from straining to see through the dark. At last I risked peeking between the waxy smooth leaves. With mixed relief and horror I glimpsed the cop, still down on his stomach, snaking toward the house.

I scanned the neighbors' yards for stealthy figures. Nothing. Although a police cruiser was parked on the other side of the block, in front of the Changs' house. Surrounded. But at least for now they were keeping back. How long that would last was anyone's bet.

You read about scenes like this in the newspaper, and you imagine all sorts of screaming and radios squawking constantly and men being deployed to cover this exit and that. But that's not how it was. Everything seemed so incredibly silent. No one said anything out loud, no one breathed. The young policeman was beyond the protection of the trees when another shot boomed out. He froze. I could make out his expression, rigid with fear and concentration. Slowly he looked back over his shoulder.

"Come back, Donaldson!" the order echoed from the other side of the road.

Looking relieved, he crept in reverse into the shelter of deeper shadows. Right away, lights shown from every direction, playing around the house foundation, across the front and side yards. I melted against the cold cement.

There's a cartoon I must've seen a hundred times. Bugs Bunny's breaking out of jail. Trapped in the searchlight from a guard tower, he launches into a song and dance routine in his striped convict's suit. Oh, how I wished I could make a joke out of this.

I let my head fall back and tried to inhale through my nose and close my mouth without clenching my teeth. Now, I decided, I have to go inside. But, how?

The front door? I wondered. No. No one thinks their father will shoot them, but as Brian had said, maybe Dad wouldn't recognize me. Even if I called out to him, if he was as freaked out as he'd been the other night in the marsh, he might believe I was the Vietnamese girl, or someone else. And the bullhorn and the cop chasing me across the front lawn obviously couldn't be reassuring him. If Dad imagined cattails in a swamp were Viet Cong soldiers, what would his brain do with armed, uniformed men staking out his house and holding his wife?

Then, I could no longer stop myself from thinking the very worst: Chrissy — and bullets. If the police stormed the place, and Chrissy got in the way . . . if the little turkey got shot . . .

Tears clogged my throat. We didn't have much of a family just now, but if Chrissy died there'd be nothing left. Zilch. *Niente. Nullo.* Zero.

Stop thinking like *that*! I ordered my brain and squeezed my eyes dry. Think how to get inside! Think!

In the winter all the windows are nailed shut for security. Most of them are too high off the ground to climb through without a ladder anyway. Windows, no good. Back door? Now, that was a possibility. The broken pane, like the living room wall, hadn't been repaired.

I crawled behind the glossy olive green leaves to the back of the house.

The door was locked, as I'd expected. Feeling in the darkness, I found the hole. But the space in the glass was smaller than I'd remembered, especially at the top where it narrowed to a slender triangular column. I took off my jacket, to reduce the bulk of my arm, and tossed it on the ground. Carefully I slid my hand, wrist, then arm through, sensing when the invisible jagged edges came too close. Slowly I felt my way down to the inside knob, then twisted the button in it.

One down. I breathed again.

The chain lock would be almost directly above. Standing on tiptoe, I felt upward along the wood until, at last, the metal links clicked against my fingernails.

My arm was beginning to numb from being up in the air so long. I fumbled with the chain and at last popped it out of the bracket.

Suddenly the lights from the road dimmed once more. That meant the police were moving again. Panicking, I drew my hand back much too fast. A glass point sliced the length of my forearm.

Muffling a whimper of pain, I stared down at my arm. A single angry red thread rose to the surface.

I clasped my hand over the deepest part of the scratch. My head spinning, I leaned against the door. After a minute I felt a bit steadier and let myself into the basement.

For a while I stood still, listening to the house above me. I didn't hear Chrissy crying — which, I thought, might be good or might not.

Then a series of low creaks crossed the exposed beams in the basement ceiling. He must have been running back and forth between the bay window in the front, where I'd seen the flashes from the Citori, and the kitchen windows overlooking the backyard.

Staying close to the open side of the stairs that over-looked the den, figuring I'd jump at the last minute if the door flew open and he rushed at me, I climbed slowly. At the top I listened for a moment before cracking the door.

The living room was pitch-black. In fact, I couldn't see a light on anywhere in the house. Was Chrissy with him, or in his own bedroom?

I stepped cautiously through the doorway.

The police searchlight, suddenly bright again through the front window, cast dense shadows across the living room carpet. Nothing moved. No sound gave away anyone's presence now.

"Dad," I called softly, not wanting to surprise him. "Where are you? Chrissy?"

Nothing.

Holding my breath, watching the dark spaces behind the chairs and couch for the slightest movement, I edged across the room. My arm hurt awfully. I clutched at it, telling myself to ignore it. The house was cold and a draft blew across the room, lifting my hair away from my face. Half of the bay window had been bashed through.

I backed away from the opening, realizing I shouldn't stand directly in front of it just in case the police thought I was Dad.

"Where are you?" I called shakily. "Daddy, please come out."

I spun toward the kitchen and — there he was.

My father was standing barely two feet behind me, the butt of the Browning Citori braced on his hip. Its barrel pointed at the ceiling.

I jumped and caught my breath. My heart was vibrating in my chest. He hadn't made a sound as he'd moved up behind me. Neither of us said anything. And I watched his eyes, searching them for a clue to where he was.

"Do you know who I am?" I asked him at last, my voice hoarse.

He smiled a little and gave me a wink. "Of course I know who you are," he said.

Suspicious, I squinted up at him and waited for him to continue. Who knew what name he'd pull out of the air?

"Josie," he murmured. "I'm glad you came home. Chrissy is in bed asleep. I was beginning to worry about you. You're late."

"Yeah." I almost chuckled out loud. Halleluia! He's in the right country, talking to the right person in the right year. Three out of three. *Fan-tas-tic!*

However, a few minutes ago he'd been spraying our front yard with buckshot. And he still sounded sort of strange, given the circumstances.

"Maybe I'd better check on Chrissy," I said carefully. "See that he's covered up good. The house is . . . umm . . . a little chilly."

"Fine idea," he agreed, actually grinning. He sat on the couch, and the long black body of the gun rested across his knees.

It was as if he had no idea the entire Groton Municipal Police force had camped outside our door, and probably every state trooper east of New Haven was hot on the way.

I had an idea. "Why don't I just . . . put the Cit away now?" I suggested casually, stepped forward to reach one hand out toward the gun. "Since we're not going to Riveredge tonight."

At once his expression flashed into alert. His hands moved to protect the gun.

I figured if I pushed he'd slip further away from reality. So I backed off and ran upstairs to find Chrissy.

171

My brother was just where Dad had said he'd be, sound asleep in his crib. I pulled the quilt down. Just to be sure, I put my hand on his little chest, and felt it rise and fall.

Relieved that he was still okay, I covered him again.

For a moment I stood in the middle of his bedroom, considering possible alternatives. I had to stay with Dad to make sure he didn't hurt anyone, or himself. But I wanted Chrissy outside with Marsha — just in case things got out of hand. Worse out of hand, that is.

Maybe I could lower Chrissy out the upstairs window at the end of a sheet rope? Or, signal for help and drop him into the arms of a cop?

But both seemed awfully risky. Too many people were standing around with guns in their hands. It was pitch-black outside when the searchlight was off, and surreal when it was on. And nobody knew who was going to do what next. Dad might see shadows and let off with the shotgun. The cops might decide to return fire, or storm the place after all. Who knew?

My arm hurt, and my head was pounding so I couldn't think. When I was unable to come up with anything close to a solution, I went back downstairs and sat beside Dad on the couch where he'd stayed since I left him.

"Marsha's outside," I said conversationally, trying to feel out the line where his reason faded.

"I know." A sad light crossed his eyes. "She won't come in here where it's safe."

I groaned. "Dad, we'd be safe out there, too. No one's going to hurt us."

He frowned disapprovingly. "*They're* sneaking around in the bushes, trying to get in."

"*Of course* they are," I snapped, no longer bothering

to hide my irritation. "You've been shooting out the window! The police are afraid somebody will get killed!"

"The police?" His voice trembled and he sounded, all of a sudden, as helpless and confused as a little kid. "No, it's too late for the police. Those bastards are coming for me — for my babies!"

I bit my lip. He was fading fast. "Dad, it's the police — not Vietnamese soldiers — on our front lawn," I said firmly. "You have to put down the gun. We have to go out there. All of us. Together."

He shook his head dismally. "No. It isn't safe. Gooks are hiding in the tunnels. Waiting." His eyes flashed anxiously between dark corners of the room. "Waiting to *get* us."

He gritted his teeth and shivered as if he were cold, although sweat trickled out of his sideburns and off his cheek; his hands convulsed on the Browning's heavy stock. Then he looked straight at me.

"I won't let them hurt you, the way I hurt their children," he said with fierce determination.

"You didn't mean to kill that girl." I tried to sound especially sure of myself, so he'd feel better. "I mean, you couldn't have *wanted* to hurt her. You're a kind person. You care about people, the way I do."

"And the others?" he asked.

I closed my eyes, feeling a wave of nausea. "What . . . others?"

He was hovering somewhere between then and now. Between Tan Son Nhut, Vietnam, and Tyler Avenue, U.S.A. And he began to talk in a rush now, as if he were afraid he wouldn't be allowed to finish.

It was so strange. For the longest time I'd tried everything to get him to talk to someone — anyone —

173

about what happened to him in Vietnam. But he'd picked this moment — when a SWAT team might break through the door any minute — to let it all out.

"Sometimes those soldiers are no more than kids," he began in a singsong voice, his eyes growing hazier. "And sometimes no one even bothers to recruit them. The Viet Cong just hand a package to a child. Tell him to deliver it to the American commander." Tears welled in his gray eyes. "Poor little kids don't know what they're doing."

"Dad," I interrupted, tugging on his arm, "don't. Think about *now*, not then." But he must not have heard me.

"Often," he continued, tears streaming down his cheeks, "often the bomb goes off before the kid lets go of it, but a lot of soldiers get hurt, too. Policy is, whoever first spots a bomb on a kid, you gotta — "

He didn't need to say another word. "Stop it!" I blurted out, jumping to my feet. My stomach heaved at the horrible images his words conjured up. "That's over. That's done with! We have to talk about *today*. What are you going to do, Dad?"

I was screaming by now. Trying to do what Whitehead said — startle him out of his flashback. But no amount of yelling seemed to affect him this time.

"I have no choice," he mumbled on. "If it's me that sees him, I got to shoot the kid before he reaches my men. Either way, the kid's dead. From the moment the VC hand him the booby trap, he's dead. That's what I tell myself. *I'm* not killing him. I'm just protecting my men."

"Dad!" He was still looking straight at me, or through me.

"I don't want to hurt them. I try to hit them so they

174

won't feel it. Just once — quick, in the heart."

I backed off a step, unable to face him any longer.

He stood up and gazed down at his hands on the gun. "Maybe it's something" — his voice cracked — "I can't help."

A soft, rubbing sound came from the second floor. I caught my breath, wondering if the police had found a way inside from an upstairs window. Then I realized Dad had heard it, too.

His head snapped up in automatic response to a foreign noise. He swung the muzzle of the Browning toward it just as I caught a glimpse of one pint-size Dr. Dentoned foot on the top stair.

"No!" I cried, throwing myself wildly at the barrel of the Browning.

The gun fired with a resounding crack before clattering against the living room wall. I landed in a heap on the floor. I wouldn't — couldn't look.

# CHAPTER TWENTY-FIVE

A HOWL, A LOT LIKE A CAT WITH HIS TAIL CAUGHT IN A door, filled the room. It was awful, earsplitting . . . but familiar and reassuring. An angry, sleepy protest. That was all. No pain, no near death agony. I began to breathe again and slowly opened my eyes.

Chrissy was sitting on a step, twisting his fists in his eye sockets, and roaring out his displeasure at being startled. The ceiling above his head was peppered with shot.

A few feet from where my father stood, the gun rested on the carpet. But he didn't reach for it. His face was pale. He dropped his face into his hands. "My God," he groaned.

Watching my father for what seemed a very long time, I tried to figure out what was going on in his skull. His eyes had become a cold gray and looked resolved, as if he'd made up his mind to do something and wouldn't let anyone, anything stop him. Drops of sweat clung to the short whiskers along his jaw. And he blinked again, and again, the way someone does to clear his vision after a photographer's flash goes off unexpectedly in his face.

"Stand over — over there," he ordered, his voice gruff, ragged. He picked up the gun and waved the muzzle indicating a place back from the door.

"Dad." My mouth barely moved, and my feet didn't at all.

"I think," he said, "I'd better go out first."

His meaning sank in slowly. Like butter melting on fresh toast. A warm glow seeped through my veins.

Chrissy tottered groggily down the stairs and climbed into my arms, whimpering.

"Shush, Chrissy. It's okay. Just a big bang." He dropped his head on my shoulder and closed his eyes, his whines subsiding. A dribble of drool oozed out between his lips at one corner.

"I'm going to throw out the Citori," Dad explained in a whisper so quiet I could only just make out the words. "Then I'll go. Don't follow too close . . . in case."

In case one of the cops freaks out and opens fire, I realized. He was trying to protect us still. Only this time he knew where we were and what was going on.

"Or, Josephine," he paused, his hand on the knob as he turned back a last time to face me, "you can wait

176

right here. Somebody will come for you. They won't hurt you — if I'm not around."

His voice sounded so sad, as if he'd just now figured out that *he*, and no one else, was the real threat to Chrissy and me. On Tyler Road in Groton, Connecticut, there was no enemy from thousands of miles and fifteen years away. And it was tearing him up because — at least at this moment — he understood how afraid I'd been of him, my own father. And how close he'd come to killing his son.

I reached out and, for a second, touched the back of his hand.

"You must hate me," he said, looking away. "Anyone who'd do what I did, you couldn't help but hate."

My throat was tight and dry; I couldn't answer, couldn't do anything but blink away tears.

Chrissy squirmed in his sleep. I hugged him tight while Dad slowly opened the front door.

There was a soft rustling sound from the bushes closest to the door. But that immediately stilled when the Citori and, by inches, Dad's arm stuck out through the opening. I shut my eyes.

The gun hit the grass with a soft thud. Then I felt the white cold of a November night against my cheeks as my father opened the door wider. When I looked, he was gone.

"Don't hurt him," I whispered into Chrissy's strawberry curls.

I listened, imagining their guns pointing at him.

He must have reached the last of the flagstones that led to the driveway when they rushed him. No one fired though.

I stepped onto the porch with Chrissy in my arms.

Everything was dreamlike out there in the green

yellow searchlight beam. But I felt as if I was breathing, really breathing, for the first time in weeks.

A huge sigh filled the night. It came all at once from behind every car and, as whispers carried the word, from neighboring lawns. Brian stood behind a cruiser, his face looking awful. So he'd know I was all right and Chrissy wasn't hurt, I flashed him an okay sign with two fingers. He spoke to the police officer beside him.

Three men had surrounded Dad. One was pulling his hand behind his back, another snapping handcuffs around his wrists. He glanced back at me and Chrissy. He didn't struggle, but I could tell by his eyes he was afraid.

People hemmed me in, shouting questions and cutting off my view of Dad as the men led him away. Somebody tried to take Chrissy away from me, but I held on to him, refusing to let go.

Suddenly I shouted over their heads. "Don't worry, Dad. I love you . . . I don't hate you. I don't hate you."

# EPILOGUE

SPRING STRETCHES OUT FOREVER IN CONNECTICUT. YOU put on shorts in May, then try a bathing suit in early June and lie on a blanket under the sun any day the temperature hits seventy. You get goose bumps instead of a tan.

Even on cold days, though, I walk on the beach — sometimes alone, sometimes with Brian or Mary Chang. Her family postponed moving after Dad was taken to the vets' hospital in Newington. That's one of the good things that has happened.

"Five days until summer vacation," says Mary.

"Yeah."

I take off my shoes and throw them up onto the dry sand, then I walk into the tiny waves until the cuffs of my jeans darken. I can hear Mary coming up behind me. She stands still and doesn't say anything for a long while. So I look around and smile to let her know I'm okay, we can talk.

"I saw him yesterday," I tell her.

She nods solemnly. "How is he?" She doesn't need to be told who we're talking about. She's a good friend.

"The doctor says he might be able to come home later in the summer, or if not then, in the fall. He has flashbacks, but much less often."

"That's good," she says.

I don't tell her that he says he still thinks of the Vietnamese girl when he sees me. I know Mary's nervous about him coming home. I wonder if she will ever come to my house after he's released.

"We're lucky to live where we do," I say from the middle of another thought.

Mary's eyes flicker up, then down to the sand. She frowns, not understanding.

"I mean, it's strange, isn't it? Depending on where you happen to be born in the world, you might grow up in the middle of a war. Ireland, South Africa, Lebanon — lots of kids are doing it these days."

She sighs. "Pretty soon it'll be in to tote a Molotov cocktail to school."

"Right." I try to make a joke of it. "Something to look forward to." Neither of us laughs.

Every once in a while I find a periwinkle washed up

in the muck. I pick it up and turn it over to see if there's a leathery black foot in the hole. If it's alive, I throw it far out into the water so the gulls won't get it.

We're alike, Dad and I, we don't like to see things die.

"I'm going to a movie tonight," Mary says softly.

I tell her that I'm working and can't go with her. Sorry.

She laughs and nudges me with her elbow. "I wasn't asking you for a date, Josephine Monroe. I'm going with Ted."

I stop walking and turn to stare at her. "Ted? Ted Murskey?"

She nods, grinning shyly. So, old Ted finally made his move. "I think he's a nice guy," I tell her.

And, of course, that brings Brian to mind, because I still believe he's just about perfect for me.

He graduated last week. In the fall he'll leave for the University of Connecticut at Storrs, which is about fifty miles away. He says he'll come home weekends, and I figure that won't be so bad, considering how little we can be together as it is.

Next year, if Marsha and I can afford it, I'll be up there, too. I expect it'll work out. The Veterans Administration sends her a check every month; some of it gets put aside for my school. I have a second job lined up for the summer, and Marsha works full-time now. She also meets with a counselor and a group of vets' wives in New London twice a week. I think that's helped her a lot.

She wanted me to go into therapy with her, but I didn't like the sound of it. I've never been able to sit in a group and talk about myself.

Reaching the hospital at Newington takes over two

hours. The day before Christmas Marsha had driven us there and we'd each given Dad a gift. I'd bought him a tiny glass dove to hang in his window. When the sun is bright, the dove's wings make rainbows across the hospital room wall. Rainbows have always made me happy; I hope they do the same for him.

In a way I'm glad he's at Newington. Right up to the end, I'd thought I could handle everything for us Monroes. I kept telling myself, "Josie, you're the only one strong enough, so you have to do it." But I guess there are times we can't handle everything on our own.

It's true — I don't hate my father. How can you hate someone who — even though he tears up your life — loves you enough to do the one thing that scares him more than anything? I think he's very brave. Braver than anyone I know.

I'm glad I don't have to worry about him, but I do miss him.

Standing here on the beach, I think of the crystal dove and squint up into the sun. Peace, I think, is a good thing.

All characters and incidents in this book are fictitious. Any resemblance to actual persons, living or dead, or events is purely coincidental. There is a Groton, Connecticut. Anyone who has been there may recognize certain landmarks in this story. But, as authors are encouraged to use their imaginations, other details have been invented that — no matter how hard you look — you'll never find.

# ABOUT THE AUTHOR

KATHRYN JENSEN spent her childhood in Swampscott, Massachusetts, and Groton, Connecticut, and received a bachelor's degree in liberal arts from the University of Connecticut. Since then she has lived and traveled in Europe as well as in the United States.

Ms. Jensen began writing *Pocket Change* when, through her husband's work for the Veterans Administration, she became aware of the number of young people who are affected by their parents' experiences in the Vietnam War.

She and her husband live in Columbia, Maryland, with their daughter and son, two dogs, and a cat.

## Other books you will enjoy,
## about real kids like you!

- ☐ MZ43124-2 **A Band of Angels** Julian F. Thompson $2.95
- ☐ MZ40515-2 **City Light** Harry Mazer $2.75
- ☐ MZ40943-3 **Fallen Angels** Walter Dean Myers $3.50
- ☐ MZ40428-8 **I Never Asked You to Understand Me** $2.75
  Barthe DeClements
- ☐ MZ41432-1 **Just a Summer Romance** Ann M. Martin $2.50
- ☐ MZ42788-1 **Last Dance** Caroline B. Cooney $2.75
- ☐ MZ33829-3 **Life Without Friends** $2.75
  Ellen Emerson White
- ☐ MZ43437-3 **A Royal Pain** Ellen Conford $2.75
- ☐ MZ42521-3 **Saturday Night** Caroline B. Cooney $2.75
- ☐ MZ40695-7 **A Semester in the Life of a Garbage** $2.75
  **Bag** Gordon Korman
- ☐ MZ41115-6 **Seventeen and In-Between** $2.50
  Barthe DeClements
- ☐ MZ41823-8 **Simon Pure** Julian F. Thompson $2.75
- ☐ MZ41838-6 **Slam Book** Ann M. Martin $2.75
- ☐ MZ43013-0 **Son of Interflux** Gordon Korman $2.75
- ☐ MZ33254-6 **Three Sisters** Norma Fox Mazer $2.50
- ☐ MZ41513-1 **The Tricksters** Margaret Mahy $2.95
- ☐ MZ42528-5 **When the Phone Rang** Harry Mazer $2.75

Available wherever you buy books . . . or use the coupon below.

Scholastic Inc.
P.O. Box 7502, 2932 East McCarty Street, Jefferson City, MO 65102
Please send me the books I have checked above. I am enclosing $ _____
(please add $2.00 to cover shipping and handling). Send check or money order—no cash or
C.O.D.'s please.

Name_____

Address_____

City_____State/Zip_____

Please allow four to six weeks for delivery Offer good in U.S.A. only. Sorry, mail order not
available to residents of Canada. Prices subject to change

PNT989

Middlebury Public Library